Susan Feldman is a Senior
Director, Alma Unit on Wom
Melbourne. she has an MA in Psycho-Social Politics. She has written government and community reports on health and welfare issues. She received a First Time Writer's Grant from Film Victoria to develop a film script. She has co-authored a book *Everybody's Business, Somebody's Life*, Federation Press (1991). Her current research, together with Barbara Kamler, focuses on providing opportunities in a workshop context for women to write stories on ageing.

Dr Barbara Kamler is a Senior Lecturer in Language Education at Deakin University. She has teaching and research interests in language and gender, discourse analysis, writing pedagogy and academic writing. She is the co-author of two books, published widely in national and international journals on gender and writing, writing and the law and writing and ageing. Her poetry has been published in *The Age, The Australian* and a number of literary journals. Barbara is editing a book, *Gender, Early Chidhood and Schooling: Critical Research Perspectives*. Her current research project, *Writing Stories of Ageing*, involves working with women 60-85 who she is encouraging to write about their experiences of ageing.

Dr Ilana Snyder is a Senior Lecturer in Language Education in the Faculty of Education at Monash University. Her research and writing focus on the of electronic reading and writing technologies and their implications for education. She has published widely in national and international journals on topic of computers and writing. She has just completed a book called *Hypertext* for Melbourne University Press.

Stories
of women
growing
older

something that happens to other people

Susan Feldman
Barbara Kamler
& Ilana Snyder

A Vintage Book
published by
Random House Australia Pty Ltd
20 Alfred Street, Milsons Point, NSW 2061

Sydney   New York   Toronto
London   Auckland   Johannesburg
and agencies throughout the world

First published in 1996

Copyright © Susan Feldman, Barbara Kamler and Ilana Snyder 1996
Copyright © in individual stories remains with the authors

All rights reserved. No part of this publication may be reproduced, stored in a retrieval system, or transmitted in any form or by any means, electronic, mechanical, photocopying, recording or otherwise, without the prior written permission of the Publisher.

National Library of Australia
Cataloguing-in-Publication Data

Something that happens to other people.

 ISBN 0 09 183334 5.

 1. Aging. 2. Aged women—Australia. I. Feldman, Susan, 1945– . II. Kamler, Barbara. III. Snyder, Ilana, 1949– .

305.26

Cover design by Yolande Gray
Typeset by DOCUPRO, Sydney
Printed by Griffin Paperbacks, Adelaide

10 9 8 7 6 5 4 3 2 1

For our mothers
Rose, Jeanne & Dulcie

Introduction ix

Contents

The Blue
GLENDA ADAMS 1

Neena's Gift
ROBERTA B. SYKES 19

Wild For Iris
GEORGIA SAVAGE 59

Crossing The Intersection
SARA DOWSE 89

Out Celebrating
ELISABETH WYNHAUSEN 115

A Midnight Confederacy
JOANNA MURRAY-SMITH 139

The Jarrah Thieves
ELIZABETH JOLLEY 165

Ageing, I Thought, Was Something That Happened To Older People
LILY BRETT 203

Introduction

Ageing happens. Inevitably. To everyone. Yet ageing is not something we talk about comfortably and our language betrays our fear. We talk about not looking our age or losing our youth. In a culture that reveres youth, it's difficult to speak of ageing positively as a time of ripening or becoming. It's something, as Lily Brett's story suggests, that we don't want to think about; something that happens to other people.

So we place it out there and leave it to the experts—to the doctors and gerontologists. And it is their images and metaphors we live with. They speak of disease and illness, aches and pains and things going wrong; ageing is about body parts wearing out and being replaced. The medical stories predominate. The setting is the nursing home or the hospital. The characters suffer dementia or Alzheimer's. The plot tells of their decline. They cannot even remember their children's names.

Increasingly, however, new stories are appearing which portray ageing as an active time when women and men can live their lives in an engaged way. The post-retirement years are represented as a time of release from the responsibilities of parenting, a time to travel and pursue new interests. Such changes are welcome, but unfortunately they are also creating impossible stereotypes which we call *super-ageing*. Newspapers are filled with photos of financially secure, fit, fabulous older people. We see grandmothers riding motorcycles in fur coats, running marathons in lycra shorts, swimming in the bracing winter sea. These images may be an antidote to the older stereotype of grey-haired, frail women staring vacantly from their wheelchairs, but they are simply a new oppression which most women don't want.

What is missing are the stories of ordinary women getting on with their lives—getting older—

getting along. Stories which show risk-taking and new challenges as well as weakness and physical deterioration. It seems to us the silences about the diverse ways in which women grow older are profound and the need for new stories as pressing as ever. This book acknowledges that need.

It had its beginning at a dinner in Melbourne in 1993 when we listened to Betty Friedan, a founding mother of contemporary feminism, speak to a large gathering about new possibilities for older women. The occasion of her visit was the opening of the Alma Unit on Women and Ageing, a teaching and research centre which Susan Feldman directs at the University of Melbourne. Ageing, Friedan argued, is too often seen as a time of loss and desolation. If it is not also understood as a time of irreverence and courage, then we do not expect such attributes in our mothers or ourselves. We fear the inevitable and grit our teeth in anticipation. Growing older is a time to dread.

After the dinner, we discussed the power of stories and the possibility of inviting both inexperienced and experienced Australian writers to take women and ageing as their theme. We believed their stories might provide new metaphors which could make a difference to the way our culture depicts older women.

Two of us began working with women in the community, all inexperienced writers, between the ages of 65 and 90. Under the sponsorship of the Alma Unit, the women wrote in workshop settings about their experiences of ageing. Their humour and compassion presented a serious challenge to common stereotypes. Consider, for example, the way one woman wrote about confronting the physical changes of ageing in a culture which values taut, unwrinkled bodies and faces.

First there is the hair. My hair is white-grey and short and therefore the timing of the haircut becomes crucial. A day too late, it looks straggly and a day too early, it's tough looking. The hair-cut needs precision timing; making appointments and then meeting that time whether you feel like it or not. One does not annoy one's hairdresser. Too much hangs on his good humour. He has such easy methods of punishing those who cross him; he holds the scissors after all. Then there is the waxing. That's a weekly affair. Nature is perverse; while other parts of the body are shedding hair at an alarming rate, the chin blooms with increasing rapidity. Where facial hair is concerned, minutes count. What in the morning appears to be virgin chin suddenly sprouts fine little ringlets by the afternoon. These little treasures require the assistance of my strongest glasses plus a proper magnifying mirror and just the right light.

One difficulty in disrupting traditional views of ageing is a tendency to oversimplify, to replace images of ugliness with beauty, weakness with courage, hopelessness with optimism, a danger highlighted by the narrator in Elisabeth Wynhausen's story. The older women we worked with refused to do this. Growing older is not something to be glorified but neither is it to be feared; there is loss and pain in ageing, they insisted, but also laughter and wisdom. Such lessons have been important to us as younger women in our late 40s and early 50s and inspired us to ask accomplished Australian writers to help us re-imagine what it means to age.

We invited the eight Australian writers in this collection to write about ageing in any way they liked: fiction, autobiography or essay. Elizabeth Jolley and Roberta Sykes have created fictional characters, both significant aunts to the younger, less experienced nephew and niece who seek their wisdom. The other six stories are more autobiographical and make use of the personal pronoun 'I', but of course we can't assume that the writers are simply writing about their own lives.

Collectively, this book is about the lived experience of growing older. The women portrayed are diverse, culturally and ethnically. They are survivors: some have lived through the Depression, others were born at its end; some have suffered poverty and discrimination, others have endured the dislocation of moving to a new country. What they all share is an understanding of ageing as an ongoing journey rather than a final destination. The mother in Sara Dowse's story travels, sails and auditions for Hollywood movies well into her seventies. The aunt in Elizabeth Jolley's story works as a savvy entrepreneur in the timber industry in Western Australia. Georgia Savage's Iris rejects the middleclass conventions she lived by as a younger woman. The Aboriginal women in Roberta Sykes' story stand defiant in the middle of the road, their arms crossed in the face of injustice. In Joanna Murray-Smith's story, the daughter who has just given birth sees her sombre mother in a new light. Lily Brett's narrator pumps iron and discovers the body she reviled in her youth. The mother and daughter in Glenda Adams' story accept loss with gentle dignity and laughter, while Elisabeth Wynhausen's narrator rails at the decline of her body and her invisibility to those younger than herself.

The stories offer moments in women's lives that disturb and unsettle, but also comfort and soothe. They do not ignore that ageing involves loss of health, loved ones, memory and sometimes mind. But they are singular in asserting that such loss is not self-defining. It is not all there is; growing older is much more than surviving the passage of time. Some of the most vivid moments in this collection live in the strong relationships portrayed between younger women and their ageing mothers or aunts. The younger woman searches or, to use Roberta Sykes' term, 'rakes' the face and soul of the woman who has slipped away from her. Other daughters express gratitude for the love they have received from their mothers; some fear passing on inadequacies to their own children. And there is the nephew who never speaks his gratitude aloud, but who knows he has been saved by his aunt's wisdom. In a number of these stories, the turning point is a quiet moment of understanding, an internal rite of passage which generates learning.

Lily Brett's humorous story, *Ageing, I Thought, Was Something that Happened to Older People*, views ageing as a process, an uncovering and regaining—through psychoanalysis, exercise, laughter and being loved. The narrator parodies herself with a self-acceptance that is both moving and funny. In *Crossing the Intersection*, Sara Dowse's narrator refuses to romanticise her mother and her reluctance to grow old. There are no illusions here about the downside of getting older; the mother is a survivor, a fighter.

Neena's Gift, by Roberta Sykes, is a story of continuity across generations of women. Neena was a powerful and heroic Aboriginal leader. Her niece, Marta, returns home to visit and experiences the poignant contrast between her now demented Aunt Neena and the once energetic 'bully' she remembers. In *The Blue*, Glenda Adams looks tenderly at the deterioration of mind that sometimes accompanies ageing. The daughter returns to Sydney to look after her mother and there revisits the past. She takes pleasure in caring for her mother who is ill while yearning for the mother she once knew.

Georgia Savage's *Wild For Iris* highlights both the continuity and difference in the way women approach ageing. Iris is irreverent and unbowed by social mores. Ev is a sensuous woman who enjoys a loving partnership with her husband Tom. Yvonne, by contrast, cannot face ageing, death or problems of any sort. The mother in Joanna Murray-Smith's *A Midnight Confederacy* is reminiscent of Yvonne in her inability to cope and grow older. This story also explores the continuity between generations with the younger narrator giving birth to her first child. In Murray-Smith's own words: 'The child ages into life. The mother ages into mothering—she is one step away from being the most recent generation, one step closer to being the last. Nothing, it seems to the narrator, is as ageing as becoming a mother—it is the most dynamic, stressful catapult away from childhood.'

In *Out Celebrating*, Elisabeth Wynhausen's fifty year-old menopausal narrator wryly describes 'growing larger and less visible at the same time'.

Her concern is with the politics of ageing and she asks who will look after us as we grow old.

Ageing is not a new theme for Elizabeth Jolley. *The Jarrah Thieves*, a story Jolley wrote more than twenty years ago, is one she selected as particularly relevant to the theme of this collection. Her story is about the wisdom that may accompany ageing— the relationship between the young man and his older, wiser, no-nonsense aunt. In Jolley's own words:

> The aunt's strength is knowing what is right in the face of the appearance of wrong. Her physical strength comes from her determination *and* her love and great feeling for a place. It seemed to me then, and the thought persists, that to have a great feeling for a piece of land, however small, and to be able to cultivate this land, is like having a gift from the earth, the air and the sky. This gift can be compared with other gifts; one such gift is the human ability to have unconditional understanding, compassion and kindness towards other people, for example as demonstrated in the behaviour of the forest workers. And, as in the case of the old woman, the aunt, it is the showing of unquestion-

ing, unconditional love for her mixed-up nephew. A possession which is both a gift for the aunt and, in turn, for her nephew.

As a collection, these stories offer only one certainty: ageing is something that happens to all of us. They detail different ways in which women can negotiate both the joys and the difficulties associated with growing older. They show us dignity in the face of loss, humour in the face of the inevitable. Whether we read these stories out loud, tell them to our children, or keep them to ourselves, they extend our understanding of what growing older involves. Most importantly, they offer respect for the spirit and determination of the older women they portray.

Susan Feldman
Barbara Kamler
Ilana Snyder,
Melbourne 1996

The Blue
GLENDA ADAMS

My mother is in bed. Today she is not sure where she is. She looks around uncertainly, frowning. It takes a moment.

Your room, I say. The floral dress on the hanger, the handbag on the doorknob, the curtains, the mango tree outside the window.

This room at the back of the house next to the kitchen used to be mine, before I left home more than thirty years ago.

I'm not myself, my mother says, a little sad, a little rueful.

She has hurt her back and is slowly recovering.

I bring her a thermos of tea and a peeled orange. I feel a tremendous pleasure doing this, setting the tray on her bedside table, arranging the plate and the cup within her reach.

Do you remember, I ask, how you used to bring us a carafe of water and a peeled orange when we were sick?

She considers my question.

When we were children, I add.

I don't remember things, she says.

Do you remember us as children? I ask.

Again she considers. I don't think I do.

She shakes her head, not remembering.

When we were sick you used to bring us snacks on a tray to last the day while you were at work.

Did I?

She was the kindest, most beautiful mother in the world. Now I want to protect this little woman sitting up in bed in the blue pyjamas inherited last year from Auntie Fran after she died. Her white hair, usually fluffy and curling around her sweet face, is lying flat against her head. It needs a shampoo.

You went away, for a long time, didn't you? my mother asks.

In the middle of the living room of my mother's cottage are four shabby cardboard boxes—my school books, photos, exam papers, childhood writing—which I packed away before leaving home. They have been stored for decades under my mother's house and now she wants to set things in order. The boxes must be sorted out, the contents either trashed or saved for more decades. But I find I am reluctant to approach them, to journey toward the uncertainty of the past.

My mother says the past becomes less important the older you get. And I have noticed that she seems to have allowed old resentments and anxieties to slip away. But now the past itself is slipping away. She cannot remember us as children.

She says the older you get the more vivid the present becomes—the blue of the sky, the sun coming through the window as you drink a hot cup of tea, a fresh muffin, the little girls in plaits manoeuvring their tricycles next door.

I pull on my long black cardigan and my beret, and I drive down to the Wing Wah fish and chip shop. My mother enjoys a piece of fish with chips, and I want to get her a treat for lunch.

I remind her that every Friday night, when she got her pay envelope, she used to take us all out for fish and chips. At least there's one night in the week I don't have to cook, she used to say.

Did I say that? she asks, frowning.

You used to work so hard, I tell her.

Did I go to work? she asks. She struggles to retrieve the memory. It was far, wasn't it? All the way across the harbour, then a tram?

Yes, I tell her, yes. When I was sick and couldn't be left home alone, you'd take me with you to the office and I'd lie on top of the cardboard boxes in the stock room, way up near the ceiling. You'd pass me a pillow and a blanket.

It was good for me to get out of the house, she says, as if that's the correct thing to say.

But I remember how hard she worked: all day at the office, travelling an hour each way, then coming home to the petty, noisy quarrels of the children, restoring the peace, cooking dinner, then on weekends doing the housework and laundry. I remember her poking the clothes in the boiling copper, then pushing them through the mangle and hauling them out to the clothesline, hanging them neatly. She was exhausted all the time.

At Wing Wah an old woman in a long, black overcoat and woollen hat sits at one of the formica tables, hunched over a plate of chips. She wears fingerless black gloves and lifts the chips one by one to her mouth. Her long hair, limp and grey, falls forward over her cheeks, hiding her face.

I step in, intending to place my order. The figure in the overcoat is vaguely familiar. She lifts her head for a moment. I recognise her. I haven't seen her or spoken to her for thirty-five years. I turn and duck out of the shop. My fleeing is an involuntary action. My feet of their own accord stop in their tracks, pivot and convey my body out the door. I bend my head, my hair falling over my face. I fix my eyes on the ground, hoping she has not recognised me.

I rush into the Hot Bread Shop and buy meat pies for lunch. My mother enjoys a hot meat pie, too.

I am rattled, and also ashamed of my cowardly action. Amy had once been a close family friend. Something happened thirty-five years ago, when I was twenty and she forty, that ended my friendship with her. I remember vowing never to have anything to do with her again. Despite the passage of so many years, the trauma has commanded my feet to get me out of Wing Wah and rush off.

something that happens to other people

But I can't remember exactly what it was that happened with Amy. I can recall with clarity many difficult moments: illnesses and deaths, terrors and disappointments, that continue to intrude into my thoughts against my will.

But I can't recall the details of what had happened with Amy. Whatever it was, it was severe enough to make me recoil at the sight of her, an old woman eating chips alone on a winter morning.

I creep back to my mother's house still in shock, more from my strange behaviour than from that figure from the past, now wrinkled, hunched and gloomy.

I heat the meat pies and bring them into my mother on a tray. Half the orange has been eaten. There's a little tea left in the cup.

I help her to a sitting position, propping her up with pillows.

Did you enjoy the orange, then? I ask, placing the lunch tray on her knees.

She slips the pie out of its foil dish and begins to cut it neatly with her knife, lifting tiny portions to her mouth with the fork.

I ask her if she wants tomato sauce on the pie.

Thank you, but I don't care for tomato sauce. She shakes her head. Or do I?

I remind her how my father used to put tomato sauce on everything—steak, sausages, eggs—and how it distressed her, especially if he brought the bottle to the table.

Really? She laughs and again shakes her head. A bottle on the table doesn't seem so important now. He was an unhappy man, wasn't he?

She looks around the room, as if he might be in a corner. I don't remember him very well, she says. I can't recall his face.

Her eyes rest on the segments of orange remaining on the plate on the bedside table.

Did I eat an orange? she queries.

I point to the segments and nod.

She smiles. And I'm sure it must have been delicious, she says.

I saw Amy, I tell her.

I am sitting on the chair balancing my plate with its meat pie.

Do I know Amy? she asks.

She was your friend. She used to come here all the time.

My mother looks puzzled. No, she says.

Red hair, down to her waist. She used to henna it. She stood out in a crowd. A bohemian.

My mother tries to remember. It's no good, she says.

I persist, mainly for my own benefit, as I try to remember what it was that Amy did that caused me to flee from the fish and chip shop. Amy often travelled abroad and used to bring her slides to show us.

I don't remember that, my mother says.

I bolted when I saw her, I tell her.

My mother pauses, then says softly: A bolt from the blue.

When I was a child, I wanted to be like Amy. A free spirit travelling the world. She showed us slides of Iceland and when we children played Countries in the back yard, I always chose to be Iceland. Once Amy showed us slides of the United States. After she left my mother whispered to me that Amy had never visited America. She must have bought the slides, or borrowed them.

Why would she lie about such a thing? I asked at the time.

To impress us, my mother replied.

But Amy had enough slides from Europe, the

the blue

Continent as we called it then, to keep us entertained and admiring. I remember that she didn't answer our questions about the American slides, but pressed on, rapidly clicking the projector controls, gorgeous images of the Grand Canyon, the Statue of Liberty, the Lincoln Memorial flashing on the living-room wall.

I remember understanding then that adults were tricky creatures, but that is not the reason I fled from her today.

Wasn't Amy very showy? my mother contributes suddenly.

Yes, I exclaim, that's her. She used to tell you that I was a spoiled child and should be made to do more around the house.

I take the lunch plates to the kitchen and throw the foil pie dishes in the rubbish bin.

Then I help my mother out of bed. She wants to walk around a bit.

As long as you're up, I say, I think I should wash your hair.

She touches her head. Didn't I wash it yesterday?

With my help she kneels on a folded towel by the bathtub. I wrap a towel around her shoulders. She gives a little shiver and grasps the corners, pulling the towel close to her like a shawl, as if she has felt some chill. Her eyes are tightly shut as she leans further forward over the tub, a tiny figure in blue, head bent, as if she is saying her prayers.

With the hose that is attached to the faucet, I wet her hair, then pour on the shampoo and gently rub her scalp, building up a lather. I am enjoying this, touching her head, massaging her scalp, feeling the bumps and hollows of the skull, at the forehead, behind the ears, at the nape.

Doesn't this feel good? I ask.

This is how she used to wash my hair when I was a child, unravelling my plaits, gently pushing my head forward over the bathtub, the gas heater flaring up as she filled a dipper with hot water and poured it over my hair. She used to give me a washcloth to press against my face to stop the soap getting in my eyes.

I get up to fetch a washcloth for her eyes. In the mirror of the medicine cabinet I catch sight of my face, a stranger with a worried look, greying hair hanging loose. She should do something about that hair, I tell the image in the glass.

My mother takes the washcloth with one hand

and raises the other, placing a finger on her crown. You've missed there, she says.

I rub the spot. Massaging her head soothes me and also makes me want to cry.

I rinse my mother's hair then gather up the towel around her shoulders, swathing her head in a turban, just as she used to do for me. She lifts her face toward me, her eyes still shut, and with the washcloth I dab at the water on her cheeks and around her eyes.

My mother sits at the table on the back porch. It is warm enough to open the window a little. A fresh towel is around her shoulders, and I stand behind her combing her hair. As I take the pink rollers and loop the white hair around them, the sun streams through a gap in the branches of the mango tree and shines on her.

She lifts her face, ringed by the pink circles of the rollers, to the sun. She pulls at the strands of hair that have caught in the comb and holding them between finger and thumb she leans forward, releasing the hair through the window. The soft, white tangle, like a feather, ascends through the branches of the mango tree.

I do it for the birds, she says. They like to gather hair for their nests.

She tilts her head and smiles, her eyebrows raised, as if she has heard someone calling.

I see her, a cloud of blue, pink and white, floating up the shaft of sunlight, while I, in my black cardigan, my hair lank and dull, am left standing alone on the porch.

My mother is in the kitchen, moving slowly, opening drawers and closing them. She has forgotten what it is she is looking for.

With my help she has taken off her pyjamas and put on her pretty floral dress. She is carrying her handbag. Her hair is dry and now curls, fluffy and airy.

She wanders into the living room and contemplates the cardboard boxes in the middle of the room.

I'm sorting through all that stuff, I explain. From the past.

We can never get rid of the past, she says, we cannot bury it because it is in us.

I move to the doorway of the living room and stand there quietly, listening.

the blue

But we do tend to modify the past, she says. To make it manageable.

I nod, a request that she continue.

Some people, women mostly, are more likely to accept that their memories and emotional responses are rational and make sense in terms of their experience. Others, usually men, tend to look away from their own experiences to something in the outside world in order to explain their memories and justify their emotional state.

What else, Mum? I ask. I am leaning forward, holding my breath, awaiting her words.

We shouldn't be so hard on ourselves, she says. When you forget something, it could be that you don't want to remember rather than forgetfulness. It is a deliberate failure to recall. You can't remember because it is too painful.

She has become, once again, the mother who advises and explains.

Repression, I contribute eagerly, then regret the intrusion of my voice.

But she is lost in her train of thought. She continues. And yet the opposite can also happen.

She is standing still in the middle of the carpet, as if about to sing. But it's also possible for painful memories to keep popping up and disturbing us, she says. Distressing memories reappear over and over, completely against our wishes. It is interesting, and also puzzling, that two opposite reactions, insistent recall and repression—and here she gives me a look, acknowledging the word I have contributed—can exist in response to trauma.

She falls silent, gazing beyond the walls of the living room.

Are you remembering something in particular? I ask.

She looks at me, surprised to find me there. You're the one with the memories, she says. I'm talking about you.

She looks back at the boxes and begins to circle them. Perhaps the story of that Amy you say you met is in these boxes of yours.

I am startled that she remembers we had been speaking of Amy and that she is speaking so clearly and at such length.

I'll sort through them this evening, I say.

Are you going away again? she asks, and wanders back into the kitchen.

Absently she presses on the pedal of the rubbish bin and the lid flies open. In the bin are the foil dishes from our meat pies. She reaches in and retrieves them.

Oh, Mum, I say, you don't need to save them.

But she washes and dries them with the tea towel, stacking one on the other.

But they come in handy, don't they? she asks, and opens the cupboard door. Inside are stacks of foil dishes, from meat pies past. She hauls them all out and places them on the counter. There must be fifty of them.

I burst into laughter, and so does she. We both laugh and laugh for what seems like minutes, crying with laughter.

Mum, I say, gasping for breath, weeping and dabbing at my eyes with the damp tea towel. Mum, you really don't need to save any more.

She gives me a look and a wide smile.

Well, she says, pausing to think. If I hadn't saved them, we wouldn't have had this good laugh together, would we?

Neena's Gift
ROBERTA B. SYKES

T he high-pitched wail of a police siren could be heard drawing closer to the Mission. Marta looked up and smiled fleetingly.

Must be that new copper, the thought flashed through her head. *What a damn ninny*.

Her glance turned towards Aunty Neena who sat slumped in her chair near the rail of the verandah. She raked her eyes over her much-loved Aunt, looking for any sign, any nervous twitch no matter how small, which might indicate that the sound of the siren had been heard and had meaning for her.

There was none. Aunty Neena gazed out towards the treetops as though absent-mindedly sorting through internal thoughts, without so much as a

something that happens to other people

flicker of eye movement or change in breathing rhythm. But the sound of the siren was coming closer, growing louder, and although the car had not yet appeared over the small crest leading into the clearing around the Mission houses, Marta could not go back to reading the book on her lap until the issues it signalled had been somehow explored and resolved.

Marta's attention was split between watching for the car's flashing beacon and keeping an eye out for any change at all in her Aunt.

Harold, and probably Joe-Boy, she thought, *that's who he's come for*.

Until then, the little Mission had reverberated with all the usual late afternoon sounds: worn balls striking handheld bats in games conducted on the only flat section of land on neutral territory, that is, in the middle of the unsealed road; youngsters' voices raised in intermittent screams of joy or despair, depending on whose side scored or missed; younger children's occasional high-pitched howls for attention; mothers and grandmothers calling hopefully to members of their broods to get chores done, wood chopped, water carried, in preparation of the evening meal. Lazy smoke drifted up from the chimneys of several houses, an indication of cooking in progress.

Suddenly, the ordinary sounds of early evening were dying in inverse proportion to the intrusion of the police siren. Heads turned and froze momentarily in the air as, ears cocked, each person estimated how far or near the police car was, how much time there was to prepare for its inevitable arrival on the scene. There was no question whether or not the police car was coming to the Mission. The narrow rutted dirt track only came to the Mission; it went no further. For vehicles, this was really the end of the line.

Almost imperceptibly, the community thinned, then disappeared. Marta watched as grown men walked rapidly and deliberately to their own houses, closing the front doors firmly behind them. Her heart ached as she registered one of the demoralising results of the long and relentless intimidation of her people. The mere sound of a police siren in the air produced an almost spiritually paralysing effect on the men in the community, though the sound was only a symbol of the injustice and cruelty it so often signified.

Most of the children, too, had 'dematerialised'.

Many were now squatting behind bushes, or peering from behind trees and around old car bodies, their eyes huge with curiosity and fear.

Out of sight, Marta's mind replayed the refrain she had heard hissed at herself and her chums throughout her own childhood every time the siren had made its approach. *Get down, girl, and don't be seen.* She heard it now in the air, whether or not she could hear it in actuality.

She glanced again at Aunty Neena, who remained sitting silently, her eyes still. A chill ran over Marta. Where was the Aunt she knew so well? What illness and trauma had driven away the woman whose strength was legendary and left this empty shell, this replica, who still looked like the familiar Neena, but so obviously was not. Could this situation not evoke even a small hissed warning from her Aunt?

In her imagination, Marta saw her Aunt rise from a chair in the kitchen and, dusting damper flour from her hands and patting them on her skirt, come through the door to lean on the pole at the corner of the verandah, her eyes brazenly taking the measure of the police car. Marta shook her head.

No, that's the Aunt of old, Marta told herself, and

her eyes confirmed that knowledge. Aunty Neena remained unmoved. Marta had been half lying across an old kapok mattress spread on an antique camp stretcher, her back propped against the wall and supported by two vinyl covered cushions. She jumped to her feet.

The flashing light popped up over the top of the small hill and the police car lurched with a crash into the depression which immediately followed. Tyres spinning and kicking up dust, the car turned sharply to the left. It would circle the small compound on the ring road in the opposite direction to that which was always used by the few Mission inhabitants who had cars and by any of the occasional visitors. Had a regular road user been on his or her way out, a head-on crash with the speeding police vehicle would have been inevitable.

Marta stood directly behind Aunty Neena, her hands resting lightly on her Aunt's shoulders, and rolled her eyes at the continuing demonstration of stupidity by whoever was driving the police car. She gently patted back a few wisps of Aunty Neena's soft grey hair which had escaped from the elastic band meant to keep it in place on the back of her neck.

It has to be that dumb fool, she thought, easily conjuring up in her head the image of the cocky young man in police uniform she had noticed in the nearby township yesterday. Her cousin, Hugh, had taken her in to get supplies, and his battered old station wagon parked in front of the store had attracted the policeman's attention. She had stood in the store's doorway as Hugh was packing their groceries into boxes, and watched while the policeman peered intently at the registration sticker. Satisfied it was in order, he had circled the car, inspecting the tread on the tyres. Finished, he returned to the back of the car where he bent forward slowly, perhaps wondering if the crack he could see in the plastic cover on one of the stoplights impaired its function and might warrant a ticket. As he straightened up, he sensed Marta's eyes on him and, glancing directly back at her, he smirked and shrugged before sauntering away. Hugh nudged her in the back with the first of the grocery boxes to indicate she should open the car's door. He muttered, as much to himself as to her, 'That must be the new cop in town everyone's talking about. They reckon he's keen on League, so he can't be too bad.' Marta had smiled to herself at this appraisal which, it had seemed to her in that moment, sounded very male and very Australian.

On their way home, Hugh had brought up the new policeman again, this time predicting the likelihood that it would be he who would come out to pick up Harold and Joe-Boy. 'He'll want an official excuse to come out to the Mish,' ventured Hugh, 'and Harold and Joe-Boy both have outstanding fines. We've been waiting. Only a matter of time.'

On the verandah, Marta's face puckered as she recalled more details of Hugh's conversation. Harold and Joe-Boy, both home between stints of fruit-picking in the orchard regions in the south of the state, had started a blue in town one night, responding to a racist comment by smashing a guy's windscreen in with their angry fists. The magistrate had been sympathetic and, not wanting to send them to gaol, had fined each a thousand dollars plus reparation. Harold and Joe-Boy, by way of reparation, had bought a second-hand windscreen in a city nearby to replace the windscreen they had broken, and contacted the owner to arrange to have it fitted. The man agreed to a meeting in the street in front of the police station, which Harold and Joe-Boy understood to mean that he was frightened of them. They loaded the windscreen into the back of Hugh's station wagon, and Hugh had driven them and it to the meeting.

The man had met them in a brand new car and told them he'd had to sell the car with the broken windscreen 'for a song', and now he didn't want reparation in the form of a windscreen, he wanted the price of a new windscreen, in cash, in his hand. Leaning against the white picket fence of the police station-cum-residence, his air had been so proprietary that Hugh had felt sure the man must have a copper somewhere for a brother, so sure was he that police interest would protect him. Harold and Joe-Boy, however, had been so incensed by his attitude because they felt he was trying to run a scam on them, that they hauled the windscreen they bought out of the back of the station wagon and tried to get the man to accept it there and then. When he refused and threatened to yell so that the police would come out of the station, Harold and Joe-Boy had picked up the windscreen and threw it in the air.

'Windscreens are such an awkward shape,' Hugh had said, laughing—and apologising for laughing at the same time—'that the old windscreen sailed through the air at such an angle and tilt and everything, ha ha ha, that it hit the windscreen of the new car he was driving and,' pausing to wipe tears of mirth from his eyes on the sleeve of his shirt as he drove, 'both windscreens ended up being busted. Completely buggered.'

Marta and Hugh had had a good laugh at this story of accident and misfortune which had left no one physically hurt, but for Harold and Joe-Boy, who hadn't the chance of a snowball in hell of paying the fine before the next picking season anyway, it had all added up to a prison stint in the offing. The old Sergeant, Toffee, hadn't come out with the warrant. Toffee was canny in the ways of the town's Aboriginal residents, and he'd left the Mission in peace over the Christmas holidays, secure in the knowledge the lads weren't going anywhere. Besides, he'd probably known the new posting was due to arrive after Christmas, and that he'd be eager to show how good he was by rounding up anyone on outstanding warrants.

Toffee'll be having a good laugh in town, right now, thought Marta. This wasn't the first 'new' man Toffee had broken in to the ways of their town. Toffee had been in place so long he was able to predict how most townspeople would respond in most circumstances with a great deal of certainty, particularly Mission people. His long 'business' association with Aunty Neena had given him that.

First on the Mission to hear a siren's approach, of course, were the dogs. Long before human ears picked up and identified the sound, the animals whimpered and slunk away, hiding under houses or old car bodies. With them had moved Harold and Joe-Boy. Naturally. By the time the police car skittered onto the Mission ring road, Harold and Joe-Boy were miles away, probably throwing their fishing lines into one of the river's few remaining summer deep-holes. They would reappear in a couple of hours, as if their sudden departure and subsequent absence had been planned as a fishing expedition and had nothing at all to do with any police visit which might have taken place while they were away. It was a long time-honoured method of saving face, about which Sergeant Toffee was well aware. His new man, of course, was not. Lesson One.

Around the other side of the Mission and out of sight from the verandah, Marta fitted the sounds she could hear to the scene she knew from experience was taking place. The siren choked to silence, probably in front of the Baileys' house, followed by the cacophony of dogs barking and a long pause before the slam of the car's door. *He tested whether the dogs were likely to bite him*, thought Marta, *before he stepped fully outside the safety of his car.* Marta knew an officer's first visit always provided crucial information for the Mission's residents, and that later, after he was gone, children would mimic and ridicule his fear if he hadn't demonstrated what they regarded as sufficient bravery. A good balance between fearlessness and foolhardiness was held in high regard. Officers who showed both at their first sighting were often thought likely to make formidable pursuers.

Marta wondered how he'd rated, length of time not being the only criterion. Her hands caressed the top of Aunty Neena's shoulders and, quite suddenly and unexpectedly, she felt tears well up in her eyes and spill over.

This wouldn't be going down like this—if Aunty Neena was her own self, she thought. Aunty Neena had broken in Sergeant Toffee and others before him. In Marta's youth, a police car, when it came out, drove onto the Mission quietly and respect-

something that happens to other people

fully, and pulled up in front of Aunty Neena's house. If the visit was to execute a long standing warrant, Toffee would have made it a point to draw Aunty Neena aside when she was in the township on pension day for groceries—to make arrangements for a suitable day and time to come out.

It hadn't always been like this, Marta reflected, and the relationship between the Mission and police had often been completely out of hand. In Aunty Neena's early days, although the Mission had been under the control of a resident white manager, rape of Mission girls by police was not an unheard-of occurrence. 'Not exactly common,' Marta had overheard Aunty Neena agree in sessions where the Elders mulled over the history of the Mission, 'but also not punished!' she had pointed out quickly and pointedly.

Marta had often wondered what unique combination of personality traits and experiences had fused to produce her Aunty Neena. As with most of the Mission's young girls, the welfare had carried Neena and her three younger sisters away. Their youngest sibling, a brother, had been inspected by the welfare and found to be either too young or too puny to be taken at the same time.

32

But Grandma Carter, as she later became known, was so overwhelmed with grief by the loss of her three oldest children that she had been unable to make the world and life sufficiently attractive to the boy and he had just withered and died. 'Like her own heart,' they said of Grandma Carter. 'It too withered and died.' She just got up every morning, did her work, looked in her Bible, and went to bed every night. That was it. No joy. No one remembers ever seeing her smile from that day on. And when her son died, she didn't even weep. That shocked everyone, because they realised that somehow she must have been expecting it. She felt that nothing good could ever happen again, and when something else bad happened, it was as though misery and grief were the stuff of life.

At Cootamundra Girls' Home, where Aboriginal girls were trained for their lifetime occupation of domestic service to white people, Neena had learned the rudiments of how English people wanted their houses cleaned and run. Although all the inmates were subjected to great hardship, and access to their family's love and Aboriginal culture was severed, an Aboriginal culture of a modified sort continued to exist and flourish. This culture was fed, in part, by each batch of new arrivals contributing their knowledge to the existing pool, as well as by their remoteness from the deeper aspects of European culture beyond the labour and supervision that learning domestic work entailed. The older Aboriginal girls, Neena amongst them, fostered this institutional Aboriginality as though it was a thin string that could be followed back to their real lives. They lovingly placed the cord into the hands of younger girls, encouraging them to hang onto it tightly, as if their lives and sanity depended on it.

Marta had also been born on the Mission, but a series of government crises in Aboriginal affairs had begun to force changes. Children of Marta's age and some slightly older walked almost two miles to the main road each morning and were picked up by bus to be transported to the nearest school. By contrast, Marta's mother, Aunty Neena's sister, and their entire generation, were barely able to form their own names in block letters as adults. Embarrassed now by the very thought of it, Marta recalled how superior she had felt to her mother when she and her friends had realised their parents were totally dependent on their reading and interpretation of notices and reports sent home from school.

From her early childhood, Marta realised, she had known nothing of Aunty Neena, apart from her occasional visits. Aunty Neena would arrive, about once a year, which she called her 'annual holidays', with suitcases laden. She had had no children herself, a fact which Marta only found remarkable once she had grown up and begun to appreciate its significance. The booty which Neena had shared with her sister, Marta's mother, and her family included many of the small items which all children find attractive, but which impoverished Aboriginal parents were normally unable to provide for their children. *The bride doll Aunty Neena brought me one year*, she thought, *made me the flashest kid here. Even the boys were jealous of me getting something quite so fab.*

When Marta was nine, Aunty Neena had given up her job as housekeeper on a rural property and moved back to the Mission. As an adult, Marta's understanding of this deed had grown. At the time, her mother's increasing illness and alcoholism, and the deteriorating state of their house, surroundings and social environment had just been facts of life.

Aunty Neena sent money to help out, but the money was misused. Eventually Aunty Neena recognised the greatest resource she could put into the community in which she had been born was her own head, heart and hands.

Although the property owners where Aunty Neena had worked had treated her well—'Far better,' she'd been fond of saying, 'than most of the other Cootamundra girls fell into,'—the government had claimed most of the wages of Aboriginal people in regular work. This money, so Neena had been told, was held by the government against her future needs, 'sort of money in the bank, and if you don't need it later, it will go to help your people.' But when the time came that Neena left the job and wanted the money within her own control, neither her employers, who had been paying the money into the government trust for years, nor personnel from the Aboriginal Welfare office could tell her the process by which she should have been able to recover her money.

Marta remembered her Aunt's fury on this subject, and, despite the authority and esteem which she had later generated for herself on the Mission locally, and even on the state and national level, she never got her own money back from this compulsory savings program. 'That . . . that hussy,' Aunty Neena would splutter, using her strongest expletive to describe the white female Aboriginal Welfare officer she'd spoken to about pursuing her funds. 'She knew the government had stolen my money—and was using it to pay *her* wages. All over this country the government was stealing our wages from us. They oughta be shamed, but they're not. They got no shame.'

So Aunty Neena had arrived back on the Mission with her suitcases and very little else. Marta recalled the sense of profound disappointment which had washed over her when she realised that, this time, her Aunt's cases contained only her own clothing and meagre chattels. And, to the children, it seemed like no time at all passed between their Aunt coming to live with them and their mother's quiet death, although she later realised it had been a year. *A good year*, Marta reflected, with memories of Aunty Neena's injection of order into their crowded household, a transition made easy and rewarding by the splendid array of food which began to routinely appear on their table and the most delicious cooking smells which wafted over the Mission in the evening—causing her family, yet again, to be the envy of the neighbours.

Whatever they taught her at Cootamundra and whatever she did in her job, reflected Marta, *my Aunt never did learn to be bowed.*

If asked when she was younger, Marta would have described Aunty Neena as a bully. Although most of the residents of the Mission were law-abiding, the majority sober, and a fair amount of standing up for themselves went on between the families, Marta and her generation were completely unused to seeing their own people go eyeball-to-eyeball with anyone outside their community, much less white authority figures. Aunty Neena, however, appeared to be wholly comfortable in her interactions with white people, and she would articulate her expectations to those white people concerned. She had always seemed to be telling people, black or white, cab-driver or copper, what to do.

When Aunty Neena had first returned, and Marta's mother was still alive, Marta had often heard her mother's sharp intake of breath at what she would, after the event, call 'your aunt's nerve.' It was thought, and often said in those early days, that Aunt Neena's nerve would end up getting them all in gaol. It seemed Aunt Neena just didn't know when to be quiet, to keep her mouth closed.

Marta could clearly recall the first time Sergeant Toffee had come to the Mission to carry out a search and cart someone off to prison. Everyone had done their disappearing act, including Marta, and Sergeant Toffee had started at one of a row of houses, loudly and brusquely calling everyone he saw to try to get them to answer to him. He swung his truncheon in his hand, perhaps to dissuade the dogs from coming too near or for more sinister reasons.

As he turned away from a house where he had made no significant progress in his quest to locate either the address of the house he was to search or the prospective prison inmate he hoped to round up, a look of surprise rippled over Toffee's face when he saw a grown black woman standing in the middle of the road. A child he may have understood, someone who hadn't yet learned their place in the scheme of things. But a woman?

He noticed her stance, firmly positioned, head facing directly at him, and her unwavering look from beneath hooded brows. Her arms were folded in front of her solid body, and it was obvious this was no accidental crossing of their paths.

Aunt Neena raised her arm and pointed at Sergeant Toffee, as if the possibility existed that he might mistake the fact that she was addressing him. 'Officer!' she called, her voice not raised but nevertheless carrying easily over the distance between them.

Sergeant Toffee stood completely still, flabbergasted for a moment, and it was obvious the control had somehow passed to Aunt Neena. Toffee looked about him, confused, suspicious, making sure this wasn't some distraction which would enable him to be ambushed. Marta and her friends, peering at this scene from the shadows beneath a low-set cottage, had raised eyebrows at each other and muffled their mouths with their hands.

The degree of shock ricocheted around the Mission, and the collective holding of breath was so complete that it felt like the whole world had stopped perfectly still for a moment. No wind whistled, no bird sang, and no dog yapped or snarled.

Aunty Neena's voice filled the void. 'Can I help you, Officer?' she asked. Although her words sounded like a question and, in other circumstances, may have conveyed an offer of voluntary assistance, it was obvious that such was not their intent. This was Aunt Neena *compelling* Sergeant Toffee to tell her his business.

Aunt Neena compelled everyone. Once word got around about how she had stood in the road and called Toffee to her ('he came up to her like a puppy,' the children laughed later, acting out the entire scene in their game), other people in town quickly assumed attitudes of politeness towards Aunty Neena and towards anyone who was with her.

News of Aunt Neena's presence, initially, was widespread and dramatic and showed itself in many small ways which impacted on Marta's life. Teachers at the school, for example, worked harder to solve problems caused by friction between the town and Mission children, increasingly fearful of a visit from Aunty Neena. Once, Marta was in town at a corner store with a group of children from the Mission when one of her companions stole a bar of chocolate and was seen doing it. The storekeeper said to the youth, 'That's okay. I know your name. Next time your Aunt Neena's in here I'll tell her about you.' The lad blushed deeply, put the chocolate bar back on the counter, and pleaded with the storekeeper not to tell on him. Marta realised then, with a shock, that some of the children of the Mission were more afraid of her Aunt than they were of the police.

Over time, Aunt Neena's reputation grew, and the degree of respect and compliance she was able to command became legendary. On the Mission, alcohol was her only opponent.

With Aunt Neena's encouragement, children applied themselves to their schoolwork and improved their grades. When they followed their noses into her kitchen to sample her endless imaginative and tasty treats after school, she talked to them in the same matter-of-fact way she did to adults, quietly letting them know she was interested in their work, talents and aspirations. Although many of the adolescents lived under almost constant threat of removal by welfare for being 'uncontrollable', the question of their acting up or misbehaving in Aunty Neena's house, or of answering her in any sort of disrespectful way, just did not arise.

Only when alcohol began to influence people's

judgement did problems occur, and even then, this was rare. Drunks knew better than to create noise, 'racket' she called it, anywhere where Aunty Neena would hear them. As the Mission was surrounded by bushlands and a river flowed within reasonable walking distance, there was no limit to alternative venues out of earshot. Although not previously in the habit of adjourning away from the community for their drinking sessions before Aunt Neena came home to live, they had adopted the custom as the least painful option. Having to deal with Aunt Neena the morning after was a nightmarish thought, the very mention of which sent males and females alike scuttling out into the warm night air. On cold nights, the code for a drinking session was 'we're lighting up the Bush Hotel', which meant a group intended to make a drinkers' campfire down by the riverside, away from where they might annoy Aunt Neena.

But the things people got up to under the influence of alcohol were the bane of Aunty Neena's life. In the town, good Mission residents were drawn, apparently, into behaviour completely outside their own characters. Aunt Neena was at a loss to understand how otherwise perfectly sensible people could voluntarily give themselves up to the loss of dignity.

'It's not,' Aunty Neena had been fond of saying, 'that I don't like a drink or I'm teetotal. I like *a* drink. But I sit down to have a cup of tea and have just one cup, and I sit down to have a beer and I have just one beer. I don't understand sitting down all day or night to guzzle tea—or beer. It's just a big waste of time.'

Marta guessed that the basic principle which had enabled Aunt Neena to find life initially bearable, then understandable, before becoming spiritually rewarding, had been discipline. She had disciplined herself not to waste time. Drinking, to her, represented firstly a huge misuse of time, and that led to other things, such as death and destruction. Aunt Neena had, since her return to the Mission, become enormously familiar with death and destruction. When Marta was still a teenager, Aunty Neena had talked about this aspect of life with her.

'Where I worked, there was death. There's always death—everywhere. There was accidental death, and death from disease and old age, and one time a son of one of my employer's neighbours even shot himself. Suicide. But that's about the total toll of it, in over twenty years. I seen more deaths in the five or six years I've been home than I saw in the whole rest of my life, God help their souls. This place has more comings and goings, deaths, off to hospitals, off to prisons, and so on, in a month of Sundays, than any reasonable sized town has in the same amount of time.'

Marta remembered clearly the sadness of her Aunt's voice as she struggled to come to grips with their problems. 'Since I been here, I've seen brother killing brother, one time with a flagon of wine crashed over the head, but every other Friday and Saturday night, brothers are killing each other—and their wives, sisters, and even their kids—by slow alcoholic poisoning. That's what your Mother died of, Marta, and I don't want you to ever forget it. That's the true way of Aboriginal culture: you see something and you learn from it and apply what you've learnt. You know your poor Mother never went into town herself, except to get food. She didn't need to. Our cousins and her friends out here, they were always happy to bring the grog to help her to poison herself to death. When she didn't have food, they didn't bring it, but when she didn't have drink, they brought it. I didn't understand then, and I don't understand now, how they could do that and still say they loved her. It's just not the Aborigine way.'

Marta came to see, over time, the huge gap between Aunty Neena's idea of 'the Aborigine way' and what people on the Mission had grown to accept as Aboriginal behaviour. A lot of Mission people, including her own relatives, were fond of evoking Aboriginality as the reason behind things they had done or events which had happened.

Marta mused over this contradiction. She knew of two cousins who had gone to gaol together, each protesting that it was their Aboriginality for which they were being imprisoned. One cousin, driving up from Sydney, had come across the site of a recent semi-trailer accident. Almost everything had been cleared away, except for the huge box trailer which still lay, on its side, in a gully beside the road. He had cautiously explored the rig, the inside of which appeared dark and empty, but when he had climbed deep inside he discovered two cartons on the floor. The cartons weren't too big, so he'd dragged them out into the light and opened them to find two barely medium-sized colour televisions. As he liked to watch football on big screens, he wasn't delighted with his find, but it wasn't 'the Aborigine way', he said, to leave good things out to be destroyed when others could use them. He later claimed to the court that he had removed the televisions for 'cultural reasons'.

When he arrived at his cousin's house on the Mission, he had given him one of the televisions. As his cousin later explained, also in court, he only took the television for 'cultural reasons', as it was against tradition to refuse to accept a gift from a cousin.

The magistrate, a very bored-looking man with a balding head and absolutely no sense of humour, sentenced the first cousin to six months in gaol for this 'opportunistic' crime. When the second cousin heard the sentence, he jumped up and soundly abused the lawyer who had urged them to plead guilty, assuring them they would only receive fines, before turning to the magistrate and laying some abuse on him also. He got all this in before the attending police had leapt up and wrestled him to the floor. The magistrate, who must surely have realised he was in no physical danger but felt compelled to save face for the police, sent them both off to gaol for the same length of time, six months.

Almost everyone but Aunty Neena thought the whole episode hilarious and had laughed themselves silly about it. Aunt Neena, conceding the ridiculousness of the story, had not been amused that they had cloaked their stupidity with the notion of Aboriginal culture. Stealing, particularly stealing from a poor man who's had an accident in his truck, was still stealing, she said, and in the old days the old men would have dealt with these cousins severely.

'But Aunty Neena,' one of their youthful defenders tried to argue, 'in the old days before these white fellas came, we didn't have no televisions. We all had the same stuff, so there wasn't anything *to* steal. How come them old men would'a hit on them cousins for stealing—them old men would'na known what stealing was!'

'What we had in those old days,' Aunty Neena explained patiently, 'was respect. Stealing's not about stealing—stealing's about not respecting someone else. You think if you steal something off somebody you're showing them the respect that's due them? Especially if that somebody's in hospital, eh? Aboriginal culture's about respect!'

Gradually, Marta's idea that her aunt was a bully had been replaced with a different view. In High School, when the students had been asked to write an essay about an Aboriginal hero, much to her teacher's annoyance Marta chose to write about her Aunt.

'I meant you to write about Pemulwuy, or Yagan, or a football or boxing champion, Marta. A hero's not someone you *know*,' Miss Parker had chided in front of the whole class.

By this time, however, Aunty Neena *was* a hero, Marta had decided. At a Police Training and Refresher Conference, Sergeant Toffee had mentioned how his relationship with Aunty Neena had brought about great changes in the way he went about policing as well as in the crime rate in the area.

'According to the records, crime's dropped almost twenty-five per cent,' Sergeant Toffee told his colleagues. 'But more importantly, we now solve more than ninety per cent of all the crimes committed in our area. No, it's not that the Aboriginal people are involved in that much crime, but when Miss Woneena Wollem lets me know definitely that no Aborigines were involved in something—I don't have to waste any time or effort following up false clues that point in that direction. Gives me more time to chase up the real culprits then, so Miss Wollem's assistance has helped increase the rate of getting white criminals before the courts too.'

An impressive record like that was too good for the Police trainers to ignore, and eventually they had asked Sergeant Toffee if his 'Woneena Wollem' was sufficiently articulate to invite to speak to cadets.

'It's *Miss* Wollem—or *Aunty* Neena,' he'd tried to warn them gently. 'Articulate? Oh, yes. I think she's got English down to a fine art.'—Which is how Marta's Aunt came to have an official car sent out regularly to pick her up from the Mission and arrange for her transport to the Police Training Academy.

Soon, Court Magistrates on the country circuit began to hear of her, and it wasn't long before a recommendation from Aunty Neena often became the difference between a prison stint and a community work order for Aboriginal offenders. As well,

Aunty Neena arranged for community work orders to be carried out around the Mission, which kept the area nice and tidy.

When Aunty Neena was nominated for a State Community Award, and won, politicians and political aspirants of all persuasions were suddenly anxious to make her acquaintance.

Since none of the many roles she played were paid positions, the Mission house that Aunty Neena had taken over from her sister, and in which she had brought up her sister's children, continued to be her home. Politicians who thought they could summon her to town quickly found out otherwise. Aunty Neena had Marta carry up an old wooden table which the Browns had left when they shifted to Redfern to be near their married daughter and their grandchildren. The table and a few solid chairs were set up on the verandah and became her Aunt's meeting area.

The little verandah office, from which she could observe all arrivals and departures from the Mission, served her well. Aunty Neena had attracted such a stream of visitors to their home that occasionally two visitors, or even sets of visitors, of differing political or ideological persuasion, rolled up to consult with Aunty Neena around the same time. As a second car came over the crest, that visitor could immediately see that a meeting was already in progress, and would wait under a tree or talk to other people until the coast was clear.

Aunty Neena had another purpose, too, for refusing to agree to attend any meetings in the town. She wanted no politician, no Minister, no television reporter, to ever be able to say they were unaware of conditions on the Mission. As a consequence, their Mission had been one of the first Aboriginal communities to which electricity had been connected. The road had been regularly graded, and there had even been talk of laying down bitumen.

The phone company had come out too, following up requests made to their Head Office, but when they found Aunty Neena reluctant to cooperate and allow them to place a phone right in her house, their enthusiasm had waned.

'Those folk can't tell me I have to have a phone,' said Aunty Neena. 'They can't tell us what to do under our own roof. They're *my* public servants, and I tell *them* what to do. They don't tell me what to do. Tch. Tch. They've forgotten their place.'

Eventually a coin operated phone box had been

erected on the Mission, Aunt Neena insisting it should be placed in a central position and not, as had been planned, right outside her door. 'Heavens, do they think I want to be hopping out of bed in the middle of the night to answer a phone I don't even want—for a phone call to anyone out here—just because I'm closest to it? Oh, no, they don't know me very well if they think that! They might get away with that sort of thing in Canberra, but they're feeble-minded if they think they'll get away with it here.'

Marta recalled these heydays, when Aunty Neena's rule had stretched far beyond the perimeter of their compound. And, painfully, she remembered her confusion as her Aunt had begun to lose, first, bits and pieces of her memory, and later, her grip on what had become her realm.

'Who's that coming now?' her Aunt would ask, and Marta initially thought it was some sort of quiz for her.

'Mr Campbell from the Water Board,' Marta would reply, recognising the car, the cautious way he approached, and his habit of parking close to a very small tree which grew near the road—just as if it was a big tree which would shade his car while he made his visit.

'Has he been here before?' Aunty Neena would peer at him in a confused sort of way as he picked his path to the front steps.

Marta's tears fell onto her Aunt's grey hair. Standing behind Aunty Neena's chair, gently stroking her Aunt's neck and shoulders, her mind had soared off in time as she waited for the new policeman to finish his inquiries on the other side of the Mission and sweep around the ring road on his way out. He would not, Marta knew, have Harold and Joe-Boy with him.

Despite Aunty Neena's worsening health, what lucid thoughts remained had all been centred on the future. Young people whose parents she had cared for then came to care for her. Marta, whom she had pushed, cajoled, stroked and encouraged to stay at school and complete her university entrance, had, she said, 'an obligation to her people to continue her schooling.' She had made it sound so formal, so necessary, that Marta had enrolled in Arts/Law, though she regretted having to leave the Mission to attend.

Holiday times, she travelled home, each time

made more distraught by Aunty Neena's deterioration. When she had completed all but one year of her law studies, and her goal was well within reach and her success assured, her Aunt's mind had gone completely, her body an empty shell. Marta's relatives had spoken to her about this when they made their weekly call from the red phone box to report on Aunty Neena's progress. Knowing it was so, however, had done little to prepare her for the shock she felt when she was unable to elicit a response from her Aunt. The hugs and gifts she gave her Aunt failed to arouse anything more than a noise, a grunt perhaps, as if even language had left her.

The sadness this all caused Marta was almost palpable. She delved around inside herself to find some of the wise sayings of Aunty Neena which might help her make sense of the tragedy playing itself out before her.

This isn't just about the end of this old lady, Marta thought. *Our loss, her death, will signal the end of an era. That's what's so sad. Where have all the strong Black women gone?*

A crow screeched and, in the next street, the sound of a car engine started up. The new policeman had been along all the houses interrogating anyone he could summon, trying to force their cooperation.

Everything's slipping back to how it was fifteen years ago, Marta mused. *Things here only improved when Aunty Neena came to stay, and now her mind's gone, the power's gone too*. All this time Sergeant Toffee had been *responding* to her Aunt, she realised. He had drawn his power from her, not the other way around.

The situation might be lost here. Toffee doesn't know how to get it up and running again. Doesn't know how to recruit someone from the Mission to set him up as part of a team.

The sound of the police car motor thrummed powerfully in the air, and Marta could hear its tyres slipping and gripping in the loose soil of the road. Although it wasn't yet dark enough to warrant it, the car's headlights were switched on and twin beams cut a swathe more through dust than darkness. Turning at the corner, she noticed the driver rev the engine and spin the wheels, spraying dirt and small stones into the air.

She didn't give it a thought as she left her Aunt's side, closed up the law book she'd been studying and laid it neatly on the end of the old camp stretcher, and walked down the steps leading out to the road.

In the road she stood firmly, where she couldn't fail to be seen. When the police car was close enough and she realised, by the change in acceleration sound, that the driver had noticed her, she raised her arm and pointed at him—as if the possibility existed that he might mistake the fact that her actions were meant for him.

The car slowed, then stopped.

Wild For Iris
GEORGIA SAVAGE

On a windy cloudless day in March, I took Anthony to Brickmakers Park in Elphin Hill. He'd had a previous outing in the wheelchair but it was my first time of pushing it. Raife, out of his head with excitement, came with us.

I've known a lot of parks, have spent tender and terrible moments in them from City Park in Launceston to mythic Kensington Gardens, where my first and maybe last love stands lightfooted on his rocky pedestal. Of all, Brickmakers is my favourite. It's big and almost bare and dogs still go there without a lead. Not that such behaviour is condoned by local authority. Indeed we had Raife's lead with us but the idea of my controlling both a wheelchair and a Great Dane-German Shepherd cross was a ridiculous one and the length of leather and nickel on Anthony's knee was our way of telling the world we knew what was what.

The wheelchair was surprisingly easy to push and the three of us flew down the hill to the tree-bordered lake in the centre of the park. First to arrive, Raife rushed in to swim with the ducks who stayed a metre or two away but otherwise ignored him. Having settled the wheelchair on the bank, I sat beside Anthony to read aloud our favourite of Kipling's *Just So Stories*. Every so often, as dogs do, Raife scrambled from the water to shake himself over us. With the story finished, it was a damp and ragged little troop that started up the slope towards the southern fence of the park.

On the way we paused to examine the Japanese-looking wind-sail and child-friendly system of locks in the channel which fed the lake. As we left them, Anthony said, 'Run, George. Go on, go fast.'

'I can't darling, it's too steep. It'd kill me.'

'No it won't. Run.'

So I did.

The path was a long one. At its top was a small coloured playground set in a sandpit about a metre deep. Another path, running from the side gate joined ours behind the playground. We were halfway up the hill when I saw a blond child in a lolly-pink crash helmet cycling towards the place where the two paths met. Surprised no doubt by the sight of a mad old gypsy bombing up the hill with a wheelchair and the most handsome dog on earth, she watched us as she pedalled.

By the time the girl had reached the playground, we were halfway up the hill. I shouted as, still watching us, she sailed gracefully over the rim of the pit and disappeared from sight.

'Jesus,' I said, then telling Raife to stay with Anthony, turned the wheelchair sideways and jammed on both its brakes. Then I really ran.

The child in the pit was on her feet and trying to stand her bike up. I jumped in to join her and having satisfied myself that she was unhurt hoisted her out. Getting the bike out was harder but on the third attempt I managed it. By the time I climbed out myself the little girl was already pedalling like mad for home.

Instead of hurrying back to Anthony, I stood, memory-swept, beside the playground. It was another windy and cloudless day. I was twelve and had just fallen from my bike in Patterson Street in Launceston. My mother, Iris, who'd been travelling in the other direction in a tram, had somehow managed to stop it so she could get off.

I saw her coming towards me. Barely five feet high, she wore a chic little hat perched above one eyebrow and the war-time dress she'd made from my father's swallow-tailed evening suit. One panel of the skirt was cut on the bias and there was fine ribbon embroidery on the sleeves.

Reaching me—I was standing by then—Iris took in my torn school tunic and my blackened and bloody knee. Grasping one handle-bar of my bike, she looked into my face. 'I don't know where you came from,' she said. 'You're such a *wild* girl.'

I had no answer and, turning from me to watch two seagulls squabbling over an abandoned sandwich on the grass in Royal Park, Iris spoke again. 'If I'd been as wild, how different my life could have been.' Her voice had changed. At the time I didn't know why but I did know she'd paid me some kind of compliment. I even knew that I must never repeat what she'd said. Not even to her.

In Brickmakers Park I couldn't remember if my mother got back on the tram, didn't even know if it had waited for her, but I do remember watching her walk away from me, tiny and slim and straight in that stunning outfit. How beautiful she was, how elegant, and all I could think was that I longed to lie beneath her heart again.

As a child I used to stand in the garden in the evenings near the America Pillar rose, with my feet among the poppies. Half hidden there I'd watch my mother inside playing the Steinway Grand she'd bought for thirty pounds from a secondhand dealer. Years later, she sold the piano for an amount which allowed her to move family, furniture and two cats to Brisbane.

In Launceston, playing Chopin nocturnes while I watched, Iris would bend and sway in the manner of concert pianists seen in films at the Plaza cinema. I knew, as children do know such things, that the bending and swaying and lifting high of hands was an indication of her wish to have a grander, more colourful life.

Iris visited the cinema at least twice a week. When I saw Woody Allen's *Purple Rose of Cairo* I thought immediately of her, not that she was ever beaten by Dad. His cruelty was more subtle. When she laughed, he'd tell her not to make such a silly

something that happens to other people

noise and when she didn't laugh would tell people she had no sense of humour.

It's easy to see now that he was frightened of losing her. And why. She was an educated woman. Dad was taken from school at the age of twelve. At eighteen he enlisted in the army. He had great charm and a marvellous sense of humour. He was always ready to play cards or charades or badminton and he kept telling me he loved me more than Iris did, then backing up the statement with a sixpenny piece. At one stage, he even suggested she might not be capable of feeling deep affection for a girl-child. Looking back, I see myself as extraordinarily naive because I accepted my father's propaganda as gospel and although I went on watching my mother in secret, I locked my heart against her and kept it locked for many years.

In 1972 when my father died, Iris moved to Southport. She was in her seventies then and on my first visit to the place, met me at the Coolangatta airport with one leg of her knickers hanging below her skirt. Embarrassed for her, I mentioned the fact as we stowed my case in the front of her VW. Laughing, she gave her waist elastic a bit of a tug. 'Don't worry, darling,' she said, 'This is the tropics. Anything goes here.'

That was the first surprise. Others came quickly. Iris was a terror on the road. She wore white driving gloves and would let no one touch her car. My bottom might be welcome on the seat but God help me if I presumed to the point of opening a door or window. I wasn't even allowed to close the door when I got out. Instead, Iris came around the back of the car at the speed of light and did it for me.

She drove at the speed of light too, giving way to no one. At one stage, I shouted at her, 'What are you doing? That bloke had right of way.'

'Don't be ridiculous, I did.'

'But you were on a red light.'

'They are for other people, not me,' she said, rapping on the windscreen with her gloved fist to let a motor cyclist know he'd displeased her.

In Southport, instead of driving along Clune Road and doing a left turn at the bottom of the street and then another as traffic signs and sanity decreed, Iris swung left into someone's garden when halfway down the hill. Hibiscus bushes shot past the window, a dog barked and a man rushed out to shake a fist. Then we were sailing across Marshall Lane and into the drive which led to her garage.

That evening, Mot Hobler, Iris's devoted friend and later mine, found me lurking among the frangipannis. 'Your mother tells me you're visiting Bob in Brisbane tomorrow.'

'We certainly are.'

'You'll go on the bus, won't you, not in the car.'

'No. I understand we're driving.'

'Then *you* must drive.'

'Iris won't let me. I've already asked.'

'Don't go then.'

Laughing, I threw a piece of frangipanni at him.

'I mean it,' he said, 'she could kill you.'

'And may do so.' I was still laughing. 'But I owe her this one.'

We stood together in the darkening garden while Mot searched my face. Finally, he said, 'You mean it, don't you?'

'Yes I do, so stop being a Jeremiah and come inside and have a brandy with us.'

In 1980 I saw my mother for the last time. She'd fallen from the front steps of her double-decker

Queensland house and was a patient in Greenslopes Hospital in Brisbane.

Meeting me at the airport, my brother Bob said, 'You mustn't be upset—Iris won't know you. She's past that.'

'Yes she will,' I told him.

At the hospital, when we reached the ward where our mother was, the Charge Sister stepped from her cubicle to say, 'Your mother won't know you, dear. Don't let yourself be upset.'

'She will, you know,' I said, walking on.

I could see Iris propped up against pillows in a bed a long way away. As I strode across what memory tells me was a wooden floor, her eyes didn't leave my face.

I could see she'd let go of the struggle of life and beneath an aureole of white curls her face was serene and more beautiful than ever.

At her bedside, overcome with emotion, all I could find to say was, 'Hallo, Cock.'

Our eyes held, then she reached for me.

'My baby, my baby, my baby, my baby.' Four times she said it and I would have driven from Moscow to Paris with her. Without brakes, without lights.

something that happens to other people

* * *

In the early 1960s, when I worked for the manufacturer of orchard sprayplants in Shepparton, one of the fitters from the factory would give me a lift to Mooroopna at the end of each day. From there I walked the last mile home. In summer I'd carry my shoes, while ten thousand cicadas zithered among the red-gums by the river and, when I drew level with the Cricketers Arms, Tom Heenan would lean out from one of the windows to hand me a seven ounce glass of Richmond beer.

Tom, my husband's best friend, ran an engineering business in the main street of Mooroopna. His wife Ev worked with him. Tall with a graceful carriage, Ev had the dark hair and high cheekbones of Ava Gardner. Indeed behind her back, some of the local residents called her Ava G. Throughout the thirty-five years I've known her, she has worn high heels and tight skirts which show her plump and silky thighs when she sits. I've seen Ev wearing high heels and a tight skirt as she loaded and unloaded machinery and while she prepared cars for duco jobs. As for Tom, when I first knew him, he wore a shirt and tie with his overalls. In later years he dispensed with the tie and finally with the overalls, wearing drill trousers instead. His hair was always immaculate. Swept back with brilliantine, it was as smooth and solid-looking as a Roman legionnaire's helmet.

During those early years, Tom and Ev lived in quarters behind the workshop. Inside the door of the living area stood a large ornamental green bottle. I remember seeing branches of crab apple in it and, in summer, a tall bouquet of Black Boy roses.

It was Ev who got me aboard the train to follow Ron when, having been injured in an industrial accident, he was taken by ambulance to Melbourne to have a frontal lobe of his brain removed. During my absence, she cared for our six year old son along with her own two boys. In doing so, she became part of my family forever and I part of hers.

Ev grew up in Ballarat where she studied to be a dancer. At nine she'd won prizes and at sixteen was giving lessons herself. She met Tom at someone's twenty-first birthday party but didn't like him. The next time they met, she fell in love.

Tom, who was born in the Goulburn Valley, left home at thirteen to carry his swag through the fruit and vegetable growing areas of northern Victoria and southern New South Wales. He told me once that setting out to fend for himself at that age seemed to him both a relief and an adventure. As the eldest of ten children he'd come to believe there could be more to life than changing the nappies of siblings and being sent barefoot to bring in the cows after dark in an area known as the home of the tiger snake.

In the early days of their marriage, the Heenans lived in St Kilda where Ev did contract sewing for a dress manufacturer and certain baby-wear boutiques. Tom, who'd found work within the engineering trade, was forced to stay there during the years of World War II. He took advantage, however, of night classes at Collingwood Technical College to gain a fitter and turner's certificate. Armed with the qualification, they moved to Mooroopna to set up the engineering business.

Fruit and farming districts are prone to cycles of financial boom and bust. In the case of the Goulburn Valley, the booms became less and the busts longer.

The Heenan workshop housed four lathes, one the largest outside the metropolitan area. In the best of the booms they were able to employ ten people but there were times when, for weeks on end, they had neither cash nor credit. Clients, also short of cash and credit, paid for jobs with bags of potatoes and cases of peaches. I saw one man settle his account with frames of wax-capped honey and a giant bunch of dahlias.

Tom's main interest was world politics. Instead of working, he'd sit for hours discussing such things as the implications of the death of Jawaharlal Nehru or the Civil Rights Act proposed by Lyndon Johnson. When holding forth on the magnitude of corporate and government skulduggery, he'd clasp his knees with his hands and laugh silently, so that his entire body shook.

The Goulburn Valley is known as one of the most conservative electorates in Australia. With the Heenan political stance being well to the Left, tumultuous arguments erupted from time to time in the workshop. Ev usually walked away from the uproar shaking her head. Her brand of politics was of the close-to-home-and-caring variety. In Mooroopna, along with Koori people, there were Italians, Turks, Germans, Jugoslavs, Celts and Greeks. Ev was forever making up food parcels for the needy among them and, at a guess, I'd say that at least thirty per cent of babies born in the district went to their Christening wrapped in one of her exquisite handmade shawls.

Both the Heenans were aware of the danger of eating the wrong kind of food but believed the quality of life mattered more. On many afternoons Ev crossed the road to buy a packet of tea and returned with a pavlova laden with cream and passionfruit. Sitting at the table between the pot-bellied stove and the battered old green dresser, she and Tom, as gleeful as a pair of kids, would eat the lot.

Perhaps because of his football-hero status, my husband Ron was more careful of his diet. Yet he was the one who died from heart disease. When that happened it was Ev who helped me through the day of his funeral and the weeks that followed.

Behind the Heenan workshop were grapevines and an old apricot tree. Ev had planted lilies and small blue-mauve irises on the south-east side. The smell of the place, a mixture of grease, oil and diesel, as well as fruit and flowers, was my favourite on Earth. Ron's overalls had smelled the same and when I moved to Queensland in the hope of making a new life, I kept returning to that smell as a horse returns to the salt-lick.

In time, Tom and Ev were old enough to claim a pension. They chose not to. Instead they went, five and a half days a week, just the two of them, to the big workshop with its old photographs and the evocative smell.

After four years at Southport, I moved to Melbourne. From there I'd drive north every so often to see the Heenans. Leaving one evening, I told them I'd be back in a fortnight but it was two years before I returned. On that trip I travelled by train and then walked around the river road where I'd gone each morning for ten years with my German Shepherd, Cynthia. In the winter light, it seemed to me that not a blade of grass had changed.

I'd passed the office of the Ardmona cannery and was close to the post office when Ev came out of their shop and began to sweep the footpath. Catching sight of me, she froze. When I was close enough, I sang out, 'That was a long two weeks.'

Her voice came back, 'One day I swear I'll kill you.' The next moment she'd flung the broom aside and was rushing to bearhug me.

In February three years ago, Ev woke to find

that Tom had died beside her in his sleep. My son, Ron, drove me to Mooroopna for the funeral. During the two hour trip we talked sometimes and sometimes we cried.

The service was held beside the open grave. Hundreds of people were there. Tom's two sons and mine were among the pallbearers. During the address, light rain, falling through the gums and wattles, perfumed the air. As the coffin was lowered, Ev faltered for a moment. A hand clasping her elbow steadied her.

At Tom's wake we met old friends, caught up on the news, learned who had given birth to twins, who had won a scholarship to London. That day I realised one disregards the rites of passage at a price. Ron's funeral had been a private one; he'd wanted that and we complied by having an unfriendly little affair which gave no feeling of a life that had been worth living so that I, at least, was left not believing he'd gone and I waited for almost twelve months to see his hand, with the little finger which had been broken and not set properly, come through the hole in the gate.

In due course Ev sold the business. In her early seventies now, she still lives in the house she shared with Tom but, these days, she works only in the Eden-like garden they created together. There, fruit trees filter the light above roses, ginger-lilies, jasmine, violets, gardenias, wisteria and many kinds of vegetable.

Early this year, Ev visited me in Melbourne, arriving with so many apples, pears and quinces jammed in with the nightdress in her suitcase that neither of us could lift it. Over morning tea, she told me that, during a recent bout of 'flu she'd been too sick to get out of bed.

'My neighbour Mavis would pop over to see me but most of the time I was alone,' she said. 'On the first morning when I was at my worst, I heard a tapping at the window behind the bed. Thinking it was Mavis, I called, "The door's open." Nothing happened except that the tapping went on. In the end, I sat up and pulled back the curtain to find a bird there. He came every day while I was sick and he more or less kept me going. After that, he disappeared.'

Ev's choice of the masculine pronoun interested me. So did the fact that the bird she described was a helmeted honey-eater. Such birds belong to a sub-species found in a small area of Gippsland but not in the Goulburn Valley.

'You know who sent it, don't you?' I said.

She smiled at me over her tea cup but didn't answer, not even when I repeated the question.

Boxes of fruit and vegetables still appear on Ev's front verandah and she receives a host of invitations from elderly men and some who are not so elderly. All are refused. When I asked her why, she said, 'I married the man I loved. It was a good marriage with marvellous sex and plenty of it. No one has that sort of luck twice.'

'You can't be sure of that.'

'Sure enough,' she said and turned the talk to other things.

Earlier this year, Ev and her lifelong friend, Muriel Wright, spent a month together in Perth where they rented an apartment and did exactly as they liked. I've seen snapshots of the trip. In one, hat brims blown back, they are riding merry-go-round horses and their laughter is the laughter of people who have moved beyond fear.

* * *

Emily Taylor is the mother-in-law of my dentist. Well, not quite. The young woman who was previously her daughter-in-law has married my dentist. There is an extraordinary bond between the two women and Emily now lives in an apartment in her ex-daughter-in-law's garden. She is in her middle sixties, with short hair and an open attractive face, bare of make-up. Her clothes are well-cut, no-nonsense jobs but much of her conversation is punctured by laughter and she is owned by a wild little dog called Basta.

Loving old dance records, cigarettes and crossword puzzles, Emily knows almost everything. If, at eleven at night, I want the name of the first person to sail over Niagara Falls in a barrel, I ring Emily.

During an afternoon of icy vodkas served in the garden, Emily told me her lack of glamour sprang from the need to reject the values of her mother, Yvonne, who had a passion for French shoes and satin underwear.

I've seen early photographs of Yvonne Taylor. A blonde, with an air of fragility and big beautiful eyes, she'd migrated from Canada at the age of seventeen, along with genteel parents and a Judy Garland personality. Over the rainbow on the outside but with some unbearable primal hurt within.

It seemed likely to me that the hurt stemmed from the fact that at sixteen she'd had a child which was handed over for adoption.

Emily didn't agree. 'It was more than that,' she said. 'Put simply, life was beyond her. She couldn't bear growing up, let alone growing old. Let me put it this way—by the time I was four, I had a child to care for and that child was my mother.'

When Emily's first *real* child was born, it was an exomphlous baby, with the intestines on the outside. She survived for only half an hour and instead of being allowed to mourn for her, Emily had to be the cushion for her mother's grief.

'I stayed with Yvonne for several weeks after leaving hospital,' she told me, 'and seemed to be forever making China tea for her or massaging her shoulders and the back of her neck. But in bed at night, with the quilt pressed tightly over my face so no one could hear, I wept and wept for my lost little baby.'

These days she makes jokes about her mother being the only woman in Australia to have eloped with a cleric, a clairvoyant and the man who looked after the primates' teeth at the Sydney Zoo. She may be stretching the truth but only a little. Yvonne

Taylor had several husbands and a dozen lovers, leaving each of them in turn because he'd failed to convince her that she'd always be young, always be loved.

Monty Taylor was Yvonne's first husband. They met at a dance hall at St Kilda when she was holidaying in Melbourne. After their marriage, the couple went to live with Monty's mother Gertrude, who owned a private hospital at Yarra Bend. She also owned a chauffeur-driven limousine.

Emily claims her only memory of her first sojourn at Yarra Bend is of a drawerful of socks. She doesn't even know whose they were. Nevertheless, she lived there until the age of six when her mother ran away with Charlie Parker, the kitchen hand, taking the child with her.

Charlie found work at the famous Lila Springs sheep-station near Bourke and the three of them settled there for what was to be the happiest time of Emily's life. Her lessons were done by correspondence but after twenty minutes or so, Yvonne, who couldn't be bothered with them, would shut the books and the child would be free to play. She climbed trees, played in the creek, watched the sheep being shorn—she even saw them being killed. Then Yvonne absconded again, this time with a real estate agent, Phil Johnson.

The newly-formed family moved to Sydney and for a short time Emily was placed in the Burnside Orphanage. When Yvonne collected her, they lived for a while in a single room, sharing a double bed. One night, the child woke to find Phil sharing it with them.

Having done well in a brief partnership with underworld figure, Sliges McGuire, Johnson set Yvonne up in a terrace house at Darling Point, where she let out rooms. Apparently her fear of ageing had already taken hold because as Emily grew taller, she was made to call her by her Christian name.

At twelve Emily was as tall as her mother, with boobs that had well and truly blossomed. That summer she woke at night to find Phil running his hand up and down her legs. She had a room of her own by then but made such a racket Yvonne came running. A week later, she was parcelled off to her father, who'd been away fighting with the army in Syria and Crete but had been invalided home.

Emily had not seen her father since leaving the hospital at Yarra Bend. She knew though that he'd had a private investigator looking for her and, on one occasion, she and her mother almost ran into Monty himself at Central Station. Catching sight of him, Yvonne rushed Emily into the baggage room, where they hid until he'd gone.

Less than a month after that near-meeting, Emily arrived at Spencer Street Station in Melbourne. She was met there by four extremely tall women, one of whom said, 'Your father went for cigarettes. Look . . . here he comes now with the chauffeur.'

Turning to see two uniformed men coming towards the group, she had to ask which one was her father.

The Taylors were flamboyant, interesting people but Emily wasn't happy with them. For years she'd had a fantasy of being knocked over on some street corner by a man who turned out to be her father. In the fantasy, the man not only looked like the Duke of Windsor when he was still Prince of Wales, he spoke like him too.

Monty Taylor was a heavy drinker. Emily hated that and, as well as blaming him for not being the Prince of Wales, she blamed him for not being Yvonne. Still feeling responsible for her mother's well-being, she kept ringing her but Yvonne seldom made a return call.

Emily was at Yarra Bend with the Taylors for almost a year and remembers being in the dining room there when news came of the bombing of Pearl Harbour by the Japanese. Soon after that her grandmother went to Puckapunyal to visit someone. Having arrived, she stepped from the limousine wearing a Persian lamb coat with a bunch of violets pinned to the lapel. She took a deep breath, exclaimed at the quality of country air and dropped dead.

Two days after what she speaks of as her grandmother's stylish exit, Emily went to live with her great-aunt Cait, who ran a private hospital at Surrey Hills. At the age of fourteen she was nursing ten old ladies in a ward of her own. Sometimes she even floated around in a veil. Such moments of glamour were not enough to compensate for emptying bedpans and washing wasted bottoms and just before Christmas she took a job on the counter at Woolworth's in Bourke Street.

When that piece of news filtered back to her mother, she came to Melbourne, as Emily had always hoped she would, and took her to Balgowrie near Wollongong where she lived with another Phil, a hotel manager this time.

Shortly after leaving Melbourne, Emily learned that while he was running for a tram, a piece of shrapnel in Monty's chest moved, piercing his heart. Less than a year later, the Phil who'd taken Yvonne to Balgowrie stopped to change a car tyre and died while doing it. With each of these deaths, Yvonne, who'd begun to use both alcohol and prescribed drugs, increased the dosages.

In her middle fifties, Yvonne moved into a nursing home. From then on, staff members kept ringing Emily to say they'd just rushed out to rescue her mother one more time from the tram track. And when she did die, they found tranquillisers sewn inside the seams of her dresses, into her bras, even inside her hats.

The day Emily and I had the vodkas in the garden, I said to her, 'Do you think your mother's fear of growing old was really a fear of death?'

Staring at a pot of Jamaican lilies, Emily said, 'It's hard to answer that but maybe so because, with each suicide attempt, she made certain beforehand that someone had been tipped-off.'

We were both silent after that and then Emily

said, 'One thing certain, you're not scared of death, are you?'

I answered slowly, 'Of course, I am. I'm scared of the act of dying because in most cases it's pretty grim. By that I mean I hope I'm lucky enough to be allowed to sit on the hospital verandah and be given cocktails of heroin and dope, the way they do in parts of America with Vietnam Vets who're already terminally ill.'

'I was asking really about what happens *afterwards*.'

'I see. Well no, Emily, I'm not frightened of that because I regard myself as a child of the universe and believe that nothing too awful can happen to me.'

'Meaning?'

'Meaning that I guess I'll just disappear and become part of some other life form. Part of the sea or maybe just something that makes the grass grow a little greener in the straight at Flemington.'

'I thought that with your Yoga and stuff you might believe in re-incarnation.'

'Em, I practise Yoga because it enables me to balance myself somewhere between the pit and the peak. It's as simple as that.'

There was a silence which I broke by saying, 'Listen, about reincarnation—I wasn't completely honest. Remember young Anthony, the boy in the wheelchair?'

'Your friend Christopher's child?'

'Yes, well I haven't told anyone but I have an extraordinarily strong memory of saying goodbye to him somewhere in the south of Europe as he rode off to war about seven hundred years ago.'

Again she searched my face. 'Did you tell him?'

'Emily, he's *eight*. If I don't understand, how could he?'

Emily went on looking at me and then she stood. 'I'll go in and get our afternoon tea and let me tell you, I've made a chocolate fudge cake which I plan to serve with raspberries and cream. What we don't eat here, you can take home.'

'So we can be sure, can't we, that my cholesterol-related reincarnation will be sooner rather than later.'

I'd expected Emily to smile or even laugh. Instead she went on looking at me before reaching out to lift and tuck into place a lock of hair which had fallen across my cheek. That done, she turned and went towards her apartment.

I stayed in the garden thinking about Anthony, who has Duchenne muscular dystrophy, a disease which strikes only boys and kills them before their teens have passed. As yet, there is no cure.

The day I took him to Brickmakers Park we went back to my place and, at the bottom of the steps, he asked if I planned to lift him out of his wheelchair and help him inside.

'Right now,' I said. 'And when we get in there, we're going to have the cushion fight of the century.'

'Are we, George? Are we really?'

'Yes. We won't even care if the ornaments fly off the mantelpiece.'

I wish you'd been there to see his face as he reached out for me.

Crossing The Intersection
SARA DOWSE

When I was a child I never believed that I would grow old, and this was the source of some sadness. I considered being old a great advantage. I remember standing on a street corner once, I must have been about three, and watching, wistfully, a woman in a fitted black suit and a pork pie hat who was crossing the road. Her hair was styled in short, carrot-coloured, marcelled waves and the hat perched on them like a bird. The road was Michigan Avenue, a boulevard with large herds of automobiles stampeding by, which came to a stop most miraculously when a light on a pole blinked red, and this woman in her chic grownup clothes was allowed to cross, on her own. Oh to be a grownup, I sighed, and I will always be a child.

When I call up that scene today I can't decide whether that woman with her pork pie hat was what I would now describe as old. I don't think she was but her manner, her dress, her walk suggested an authority that came with age. My three-year-old's perception was utterly skewed by what I'd experienced of the battles between grownups and children, in which the former were forever trying to make the latter do things they didn't want to do and were forever succeeding. But in a sense I'd got it right. Looking back, it seems that in those days the subtle gradations between youth and age weren't so active; once a woman or man took on adult responsibilities they were old. They graduated to a higher order of being.

Their dress was different, and didn't change much from then on. Dress was far more formal then. A woman of twenty was just as likely to wear a suit with gloves as her dowager aunt; women of all ages wore sleeveless gowns with pearls in the evening—when they could afford it. Men, when they could afford it, wore suits and fedoras, whereas boys wore knickerbockers, a strange sort of trouser that came down to the knee. Girls wore short dresses with little puffed sleeves.

This was Chicago in the 1940s, on the cusp between the Great Depression and America's entering the Second World War. I'm not so sure it was a good time to be a child, or an adult for that matter, but as a child, of course, I was unlikely to see that. My world was surrounded by restrictions. The winter for the most part kept you inside; the wind that roared like a lion off Lake Superior could lift up fully grown people and slam them against the sides of buildings with its paw; when the weather was calmer we children were encased in snow suits, diabolic affairs that took hours to get into and get off. Worse were the dressier woollen leggings which were worn by girls under their coats and worked against any freedom of movement. There was also a belief that children's ankles needed supporting—my tall, stiff, leather clodhoppers took an eternity to lace and unlace, and when they were on it was impossible to wriggle my toes. I used to watch the women in their high-heeled pumps and stockings with a passionate, teeth-grinding envy, never dreaming that their shoes were even more uncomfortable than mine.

If I seem to be putting undue emphasis on dress this is only because even then I realised that dress was a kind of code, more a statement about status than it was about personality, and that for children there was even less latitude for individual expression. But it was not only clothes that bound and marked us. There was food. I was one of those fortunate children who had plenty to eat; the problem was I didn't like it. I was made to sit at the table for hours while chops and mashed potatoes congealed into ugly cold blobs on my plate, until my mother gave in and reluctantly took it away. 'Think of the starving children in China,' she would admonish, but I couldn't work out why if Chinese children were starving she was giving the food to me.

I had just turned three when the Japanese bombed Pearl Harbor and America entered the war. One of the worst things about wars is the way in which they improve some people's fortunes. While other people get injured and killed and endure the most horrible privations, some, at home, benefit from the boom in the economy, and nobody more so, it's been argued, than women. The war brought my mother and me to New York, and there were changes for both of us. My mother was working harder than ever and had less time to fuss about what I wore and ate. I was in kindergarten now, and took the bus, unaccompanied, along Madison Avenue, got off at 85th Street and walked another block to school. This was a marvellous freedom for me, and my mother gained more freedom too. Perhaps there was something about these heady new experiences that made us both revise our attitudes towards youth and age and, as usually happens, we were not alone in this; what seemed to be a personal, most private, even secret phenomenon, was in fact a social movement, or trend.

Men had always valued youth in women, but I, with my peculiar child's eye view of things, was not to know this. Besides, as I've said, there were many compensations in being older. A woman like my great-grandmother, for example, acquired considerable standing at the centre of her large, extended family. Though this was undoubtedly changing—the Depression and the war accelerated the fragmenting of families that is such a feature of modern life—there was at least some cachet attached to the experienced, sophisticated woman. The comics I read during this period (I was now about six or seven) reflected this. There was *Brenda Starr*, the glamorous reporter; for the less soignee, there was *Tillie the Toiler*, someone like today's Roseanne; and there was *Wonder Woman*.

Yet there was something further about each of these characters that was noteworthy. Apart from being strong, independent women who were cutting a swathe in the world, what was remarkable about them was their bodies. Unlike Little Orphan Annie or Nancy in *Nancy and Sluggo*, these were women, with 'fully-developed' figures, and I began to understand that there was a premium on a certain kind of body, particularly one with large breasts. The wartime pinups of Betty Grable and Rita Hayworth, the 'Petty Girl' drawings, only accentuated this. Long legs and big breasts, I began to see, had value beyond any sort of authority my great-grandmother could summon; there was something special, I saw, in being mature but not old.

Just exactly when this change took place in my perception of things I can't say. Like most changes, I suppose, it was gradual, with one world view overlapping another until one day the earlier one, like the ghost of some past self, had vanished.

The war ended and my mother remarried and like

many a post-war family, my mother, my stepfather and I moved out west, to start life anew. Now perhaps is the moment for a break in the narrative, to explain what it was that my mother had worked so hard at during the war. My mother, who was short and very pretty, with large green eyes and reddish hair and the kind of electric magnetism that made her seem to crackle when she moved, was an actor (or actress, as she was happy to call herself then). Her first love had been the theatre but she made a living playing in the radio serials, a career move that took her further and further from the stage. On radio, voice, as you would guess, was everything, but because it was a relatively new medium, people used to dress up to perform, exactly as they might have if there had been an audience to see them, which there sometimes was. For the daytime serials—the soaps—it was the usual high heels and suits, but evening dress at the mike was *de rigeur* after dark. It was as though the actors, and the producers and the directors who put them through their paces, couldn't bring themselves to believe that the radio waves that carried their voices into millions of living rooms stopped there, and that somewhere, somehow, their images as well would sneak through. They knew about television but it didn't seem such a good investment while the war was on—it was four years after it ended that television took off in the States. So even though my mother worked in radio and her audiences across the country never saw her except in publicity shots, she felt that her livelihood depended on her looks, a realistic appraisal that would only be reinforced in Hollywood.

Yet despite the freedom she'd tasted, my mother, like many women of her generation, felt guilty about the way she had raised me, which out of necessity failed to conform to the model of the family suddenly and vehemently purveyed once the armies of men were demobilised. And because of this she decided she was not going to work and would be dependent on my stepfather's earnings. My stepfather was a radio scriptwriter, making excellent money on a crime series entitled, ominously enough, *This is Your FBI*, and also had the promise of film work. But any hopes that he and my mother had about finding the good life out west were blasted with the rise of the Cold War and the House Un-American Activities Committee's investigation into the movie industry. Because my mother had been, for a brief spell, a communist, my stepfather lost his job and the two of them were blacklisted, and so began the process of despair and recrimination that would eventually, more than a decade later, blow them apart. All the while my own maturation proceeded and, as far as they could, my parents spared me from the worst of their misfortune.

But certain words, certain sights impressed themselves on me. The first thing I noticed was that my mother, the woman who dressed up to stand before a radio mike, 'let herself go', and never put anything on but a tee-shirt and shorts. She pushed a trolley in the local supermarket in this outfit, tossing in random items with a disconsolate, desultory air. For dinner we had nothing but hamburgers. My stepfather, likewise, sat in his boxer shorts at his typewriter, staring day after day at the same blank piece of paper he'd rolled into the carriage. It was as though the beauty of Southern California—the balmy climate and the giant eucalypts, the palms and the oleander, the smell of cut lawns and salt from the sea—had been permanently blighted, and as if to give physical expression to this, smog, which had never before made its appearance in that city, began its suffocating spread over the basin of Los Angeles.

My mother felt she was ageing, and for her there was nothing good about it. Time, instead of adding lustre, was closing in. She lamented her grandmother, 'old at 35'—there was none of that reverence for a life honorably fulfilled with which in earlier, more beneficent times she spoke about my great-grandmother. She wept, and after a while didn't bother to try to hide it. At the same time she started to put padding in her bras, a discreet half-moon in each cup, and didn't bother to hide this either. I saw these new apparatuses in the piles of folded laundry on top of the dryer. Most surprising of all, she began to envy me. She hated it when I went out at night on dates, made critical remarks about my posture or my hair, remarks that made a far greater impact somehow than her more frequent reassurances and compliments. It was cruel of her, but I could be cruel too: once, when she was being particularly unreasonable, I muttered to a girlfriend, 'Don't mind her—she's going through the menopause.' This wasn't true at all and it's a mystery how I even thought to say it, but it was meant to hurt. Though I muttered it in my bedroom, I knew enough about acting to make it loud enough for her to hear; she came rushing in, white with anger, and denied it most passionately.

Did my mother feel that life was passing her by? The good things about living anyway? No one asked my parents to parties, they were pariahs, their once lively social life was defunct. I now know that my mother was a highly-sexed woman, whose sexuality, because of my stepfather's own traumas, was largely repressed; and their social exclusion deprived her of the flirtations which might have kept intact her sense of herself as a sexually desirable woman. And there was also, in her case, the matter of work.

After the worst of the Cold War witchhunts had passed and the bans had been lifted, my mother got parts in some Z-grade horror pictures. She was in her forties. In those days it was hard for an actress that age to get work: the 1950s was a conservative decade, the life women led during the war, in which they gained all kinds of experience, had contracted, and the movies reflected this. The roles women played were romanticised versions of the ones they were restricted to in real life—young and beautiful, or sexy; wives or girlfriends, sidekicks or secretaries—and parts for older women were rare. My mother played a nice high school teacher in *I Was a Teenage Werewolf* who is distressed to see the football hero turn into a werewolf; in *Blood of Dracula* she was the chemistry teacher who turns a girl student into a werewolf (not a vampire—we don't look for accuracy in these movies). For over a decade she played bit parts on television—hotel desk clerks, accident witnesses, a succession of prison warders and nurses—until she landed a long-running one as a patient in *General Hospital*. By that time I was living in Australia, and I used to get surreal letters from her telling me her condition was terminal, though she hoped she would last until Christmas, so she could send presents to my children. By that time too she had left my stepfather but money was still a problem, if sex no longer was. My mother, in her late fifties, rediscovered it, and enjoyed liaisons well into her seventies, when both the parts and her love life began to dry up.

But I am running ahead of myself here, because those years—my mother's sixties and seventies—could be deemed her best. An actor's life is precarious, work is irregular, but the money when it does come is good. My mother learned to make efficient use of her down time with the funds she'd accumulate when working. She bought a house in a rundown neighborhood near the beach, and remodelled it herself; and as these things happen the value of this property increased exponentially as the area, once shunned, became gentrified. She bought a small sailboat (a 22-footer) and on weekends sailed it alone, up and down the coast, or across the San Pedro Channel to the island of Santa Catalina. She travelled to Europe, to China, to Australia to see me and the children. The rivalry I'd felt as a teenager was gone, and it was easy to see why—my mother was living her own life well.

My mother's example couldn't fail to hearten me. While the mothers of some of my friends subsided into a quiet acceptance of yet a further set of limitations (their husbands' retirements or their own advancing senility) my mother was as active as she'd ever been—and more. She had mellowed, too, was no longer the angry, disappointed person I'd known her to be in my teens. She climbed a mountain, rode a bicycle, sailed a boat, entertained lovers, went to work and finally did some acting on the stage again. Watching her, even from a distance, made any qualms I had about getting old myself evaporate. Old age seemed a time of liberation, of release from the demands of a family, with no cessation of productive work.

But there was a shadow side to this. My mother's activities had a frantic cast, as though by her actions she could stave off time. For all her vitality she didn't like being old, and said so, continuously. Everything she did was a refusal of the certainty of infirmity and death, so they haunted her, like the shadowy shapes of sharks swimming alongside her boat. She didn't like to be among old people, she sought the company of the young. Sex was more important to her than companionship; she would resist attempts of friends and relations to introduce her to men her own age, for fear she would end up some old man's nurse. To be fair, most men of her generation were grievously patriarchal towards women, either arrogant or dependent—signs of the same condition. So she knew she was in for no bargain, but there was always the possibility that she might meet someone different or, if not exactly different, one in whom these postures were less marked. Nor could it be said that this policy of hers did much for her ego. One bed partner left her when he discovered that she didn't have all her own teeth; another gave up on her when his own sexual powers began to wane.

On one of her many visits to Australia I picked up my mother at the train she'd taken from Sydney to Canberra. The trip across the Pacific was an arduous one and it might have been better had I picked her up in Sydney, but the point is that because of her previous zest and persistent, fervent denials, the fact that she *was* getting old took me as much by surprise as it depressed and irritated her. 'I have so many wrinkles,' was the first thing she said after she stepped off the train.

She was giving in. Over a decade before she'd had triple bypass surgery after a thrombosis was discovered. The operation solved the immediate problem but did not relieve her entirely from coronary distress, and she never went anywhere without a capsule of nitroglycerine for emergencies. What's more, to construct the bypass the surgeon had taken a piece of the artery from her inner thigh, and she was convinced that it was this that reduced the muscle tone there, and thus her desirability. She lamented its passing and spoke of real loneliness: 'I wish that just once, someone would put his arms around me, tell me he loved me, and hold me.' She was still bleaching her hair, but eventually accepted my carefully tendered advice about letting it go grey. It was a soft grey, much less harsh on her face.

Whatever you can say about contemporary society, it is one that puts a premium on youth, and nowhere more so than in the city my mother lives in and the profession she has practised, now for over 60 years. In the entertainment industry the aged are tolerated only if they are rich, and even the young are pressured to submit to all manner of dangerous, painful procedures to improve their appearance. Oddly, in all the time I've known her, I have never thought to ask *why* my mother wanted to be an actor—I only know that for as long as she can remember she wanted to be one. Now I speculate. Actors, like writers, are interested in people, in what makes them tick, and, like writers, draw upon their hidden selves in order to create characters. More than this, and perhaps more importantly, the acting, as the writing, allows for the expression of these hidden selves. Conversely, one can argue, actors and writers can hide behind their characters, so a kind of shyness is what draws people to these professions. But for actors these strategies are never entirely unsuccessful, for the simple reason that actors are by necessity *seen*, and in Hollywood, except for a handful of character actors, they are required to be beautiful, and being beautiful means looking young. My mother has railed against this—her rationale for bleaching her hair was that grey hair made her invisible—yet something, some basic inner integrity, I like to think, has prevented her from taking the route that so many other actors take as a matter of routine. She has never had a face lift, an eye tuck, a 'wattlectomy' or liposuction. I don't think she's ever had so much as a facial, and she's never been to a health farm. She's talked about doing these things, but somehow never got around to it. I guess what I'm saying is that, living and working in the place she has, at the time she has, she could hardly help being influenced by its *zeitgeist*. What's amazing is how much of it she's resisted.

When my mother reached her late seventies she was no longer able to pretend that life would be much different, and acknowledged that any changes in store for her were bound to be for the worse. For the aged, it seems, the myth of progress is exposed. She began to have trouble with her liver.

This was because, years before, while remodelling her house, she contracted chemical hepatitis from using too much paint stripper in too confined a space. The irony is that my mother, who never had more than a sociable drink—a glass of wine or, rarely, a martini—now added cirrhosis of the liver to her heart disease, and loss of weight to her shrinking height. She was also susceptible to bronchitis and pneumonia. After a long period of not working she got a part on a soap produced by an Australian company that had set up shop in LA. It was a terrible show, a remake of an earlier one about women prisoners in which my mother played an incurable kleptomaniac, but it provided her with the first steady work in years; and it was while they were shooting that my mother had the mammogram that picked up the cancer in her left breast. She was given the option of keeping the breast with protracted and debilitating radiotherapy which would have forced her to leave the series, or having it removed. She chose the latter. 'At my age,' she said, 'who's going to look?'

The series eventually ended (its duration a surprise to many) and my mother has not had any work that I know of since. She goes on 'cattle calls'. These occur whenever a part comes up, usually in a commercial, occasionally in something more substantial, and every female actor over 70 turns up to audition for it. There aren't too many of these parts but too many female actors over 70—the law of supply and demand can be a dismal proposition. Over the years the women who show up at these auditions have come to know one another—they are social occasions as much as anything else. The women swap industry gossip, ask each other the inevitable questions about their health, and speculate on the next time they'll meet. The friendship, however, never wholly eclipses their rivalry, which is, of course, the reason for their meeting. Now and then one of them will have a run of luck, but for some time this hasn't been my mother. She often gets praised and frequently only just misses out, for even at this age actors are chosen less for their ability and more for how they look, though now they're often called upon to look old. All in all, a dispiriting business, but I will really start worrying when my mother stops turning up at the cattle calls.

The paradox of life is that we are important and yet not important; the task we have is getting the balance right; the greatest aid in this is humour. My mother has always had a terrific sense of humour and whenever we're together both of us are usually overcome by paroxysms of laughter. Yet paradoxically, again, there is no humour without pathos, and she's had her share of that. For some, far too many, the line is crossed into tragedy; there is no justice in this that I can see, and no easy remedy. But growing old and all its attendant difficulties is something that happens to all of us—if we are lucky. Most people prefer it to the alternative.

We all teach each other, mostly by example. I often thought I became a writer because I didn't want to be an actor like my mother, because I didn't want my livelihood to depend on how I looked. I believed, with all the intolerance of the young, that one should 'age with grace', and that ageing would not be the problem for me that it has been for my mother. The joke is on me. The publishing game is a media operation like any other, and writers have come to be performers. Moreover, it is increasingly an advantage to be young. I worry almost as much as she has about whether to have cosmetic surgery, about what to wear on promotion tours, about whether to 'dress my age' or wear what I feel comfortable in. When my second relationship of nearly twenty years broke up a couple of years ago the prospect of being without loving sex was appalling to me, notwithstanding the troubles I'd had in the relationship and the freedom I gained getting out of it. I was conscious that I was not the kid I once was, conscious of the statistics which all too bleakly show the chances we older women have in finding partners, conscious too about the slim possibility of supporting myself in anything like the comfort one might hope for in old age; we writers have not been nearly as effective as actors in establishing superannuation schemes for ourselves. But what we do have is stories, and stories are the source of wisdom and hope.

My mother's life has been full of stories, this has been her gift. As a writer I could work on the material she has given me for the rest of my days: stories about the American midwest during the Depression, stories about radio, stories about New York and Hollywood, and the politics of the 50s. Best of all is her story; the story of a woman with a robust talent for living; a strong sense of herself as an independent, worthwhile human being; and an ability—most of the time—to laugh. My mother's story flies in the face of the grey, unrelenting statistics, as I suspect the stories of many women do—the trouble with statistics, and the mentality which ascribes to them such significance, is that they render us incapable of seeing, we lose sight of the trees for the wood. And the task of each tree is to grow. I have not wanted to live my mother's life—there are things about the plot and some of the minor characters I'd reject—but it has given me the courage to grapple with some stories of my own.

I don't think my mother was there that day I stood on the corner of Michigan and Superior in Chicago, watching the woman in the pork pie hat cross the road. I don't remember her being there. I remember the fumes of the traffic, the sweet, pungent smell of exhaust that I was particularly fond of, and may indeed have been responsible for my love of street corners as a child. In my own mind, the moment of the woman's crossing, the particular rhythm of her stride, the bounce of the hat on her curls, has been extracted from time, like a scene from a motion picture that for some reason or other is played and played again, as if the projector got stuck. Now that I am older myself than this woman was then, it seems odd to me when I think of it that I am also still that child. And more than this, it seems both right and good.

Out Celebrating
ELISABETH WYNHAUSEN

It was like stepping through a door and hearing it slam shut behind you. Come to think of it I was going through a door, into the Driveway Hotel in Darwin. The original driveway had been blue-lit and turned into a tropical cement version of a fern bar, with chrome and black barstools and fronds shuddering in the sultry heat.

Drawn by this vision I walked up the drive and was just stepping inside when a nondescript man asked if I were buying a drink. He stood in the entrance, like a bouncer enforcing a dress code, but this seemed improbable in Darwin, where so many men had thongs fused to their feet; in any case, he had spoken softly, in an overfamiliar tone. Of course I was buying a drink, I snapped, at once flattered and insulted, and he fell back as if I had pushed him.

Suddenly he was at my elbow again, but his manner had changed, and he was appealing to me as an older relation or something.

'I'm supposed to be meeting somebody,' he said, clearly hoping to make amends because I had misinterpreted his intention. 'On the phone she said she had a limp.' His tone became more beseeching still. 'You wouldn't believe the number of people with a limp who've come in here tonight,' he said.

Other women complained they grew invisible by degrees once they reached their forties. Not being a beauty, I'd always felt myself to be more audible than visible, but it hardly lessened the shock of being perceived as a limp in female form.

I suppose I'd had a glimmer of an idea about getting into trouble one last time in the tropics. But it seemed to be too late, even in Darwin, where men outnumbered women and a woman on her own walking down a city street at night remained an object of ribald speculation. The door had slammed shut.

* * *

I know some women who deny they're middle-aged until they're fifty-something, but I leaped into declarative middle age about two minutes after my fortieth birthday. Of course I wouldn't have done so if I thought I looked middle-aged, like a spinster in a Barbara Pym novel, prematurely rolled in a cardigan. I liked to think I looked sort of young for my age. I was amazed when people failed to remark on it, and irritated when they reacted, as if I had confirmed the obvious.

Now I am middle-aged, I find it no easier to tether its meanings than to reconcile the inner self with the outer reflection. But I can report a positive indicator of the approaching half-century, at least for women who don't have a man in their lives.

There comes a day when they fail to mention this fact in the daily conversations with their girlfriends. I first noticed it a couple of years ago. Gone as if surgically excised was the chorus of complaint, the confusion and sense of loss that had followed the realisation that there weren't any independent men looking for the likes of us. We hadn't touched on the subject for months. What we talked about as routinely as we once talked about the absence of men was the presence of food.

We were fixated on food, but no more so than the long-married women of my acquaintance. All spoke so constantly and so hungrily about food that it was almost as if we were starved of something, even as we complained about putting on weight.

Nor was it just us. In a newspaper interview a couple of years ago, a man who owns a boutique in Sydney's Double Bay, contended (a bit unwisely, one might have thought), that most of his middle-aged customers had gone up a size. I, too, have gone up a size, a couple of years after giving up smoking and transferring the allegiance—and more than an element of the compulsiveness—to food. Instead of cruising around late at night looking for an open milk bar because I had only half a pack of cigarettes to last until morning, I'd consider what food there was in the fridge, and whether I ought to stop for a little something to fill in the long hours between dinner and breakfast.

I fantasised about food. I pause and realise I've used the past tense, as if to suggest I've conquered this unseemly lust. The fact is I find my mouth watering as I mention conversations about food—

conversations that with their emblematic exchanges of recipes and diet tips tend to follow a pattern that ends in intimate confessions of shared weakness. But behind the ritual niceties are the humiliating realities.

I work in the Sydney headquarters of News Ltd, a dump with a canteen that has food so inferior you feel a lesser person just looking at it. And yet mortifying as it is to admit, I'll eat there (drowned coleslaw, ochreous macaroni salad) rather than missing a meal. I always feel furtive about it, too, as if I'll be caught out, eating again. I tell all this to a close friend, who laughs in understanding.

She is someone who gives visitors something good to eat even if they've dropped in for a hurried business discussion. But no sooner have the people who dropped in that day left, she admits, than she tidies up the dishes, looks around her beautiful, empty apartment and then, without so much as a conscious thought, dives into the nut jar.

* * *

It happened the month—the same bloody month— that I began work for the *Australian* newspaper. I had been a journalist for half my life but had freelanced for many years, and it was to take me some time to adjust to working in a newspaper office again. The editorial floor of the *Australian* is in a room so vast that the thin rays of light from the windows at one end of the room can't be seen at the other.

The first glimpses of the place filled me with much the same sense of horror as would have been engendered by the first glimpses of a cotton gin or an auto assembly line. Legions of pale, silent people sat staring fixedly at their computers. When I last worked in a big newspaper office, people had clattered away companionably on typewriters. The reporters at the *Australian* would have been in primary school then. It was soon obvious, in fact, that the frequent jokes one made about one's advanced age didn't sound like jokes to colleagues young enough to be one's children. And the joke was on me.

I hadn't been there a month when I had the first hot flushes. They arrived one day like a bolt from the blue. I knew what had happened but I couldn't get used to the idea. Otherwise so inclined to expose my frailties that I'd blurt out my age, as I used to blurt out I was Jewish (sensing it to be an unresolved issue, not least for me), I decided there wasn't any immediate need to inform people half my age that I was menopausal. I was a shade less restrained outside the office.

'I've started a new job and started menopause, all at once,' I wailed to anyone who'd listen. My dentist, my doctor, my hairdresser, my friends. The whole thing seemed improbable. I didn't so much have a premonition of mortality as a feeling that someone, somewhere, must have made a mistake. I felt like shouting that I wasn't ready.

I dare say this response was no more than was expected of members of my generation. The thirty-somethings I worked with were convinced that the forty-somethings who had been at high school and university in the nineteen-sixties were spoiled.

It would have confirmed their suspicions to hear that I was having a bit of trouble coming to terms with the big M. Though speaking as someone born in June, 'forty six, almost the first month of the baby boom, I'm inclined to think that it's the women born the previous decade who set about reinterpreting the change of life with such vigour, at a time the subject was barely mentioned in polite society, let alone discussed ad nauseam.

I was to do my bit, after trying hormone replacement therapy. I took it because I was anxious about the new job but found its effects disconcerting. First my breasts blew up until it seemed someone had been at them with a bicycle pump. Next my libido acted up as it last had when I was fifteen. If I didn't know what to make of it then, there didn't seem to be much to do about it now.

On the beach in the mornings, I stared lasciviously at the bodies of young men, who ran past me, unseeing. I happen to turn my feet outwards, like a duck going faster than usual. If the bronzed young men were jogging alongside bronzed young women, I'd grow visible for a moment as one or other, probably the woman, drew quick, covert attention to the spectacle before them. It might provoke them to smile at each other, the source of their amusement already forgotten in their pleasure at their own bodies and their own strength and beauty. I could accept that. What bothered me was that for several days a month, I remained in an uninvited state of incipient arousal, ready to jump on a doorknob, as I insisted on putting it during one of the arguments about HRT.

The women I knew seemed strangely sanguine about hormone replacement therapy. They spoke as if it were as natural to reach for the oestrogen and progesterone as for aspirin or even Dettol—something one did without giving it another thought. One old friend recommended HRT if I were more disagreeable than usual, another had convinced herself there wasn't a reason for a woman to experience so much as a hot flush, a third confessed that her husband insisted she took it because it made her even-tempered.

But I had talked myself out of it. Though hormone replacement therapy had been around for years, I couldn't help feeling that its sudden widespread popularity was somehow suspect. It was as if it were the correlative of the baby boomer sense of primacy. Just as we refused to step aside for the thirty-somethings coming along behind, so we refused to accept the physiological limitations of age. The generation that had once flattered itself on facing up to the brute facts of life was now ducking and weaving all over the place in its attempts to modify the meanings of ageing—should preventing the process prove impossible. It came to me one day that taking HRT was like swallowing some elixir of youth, and I gave it up.

Back came the hot flushes. I had lost all reluctance to explain the situation to my colleagues by then. They would have known something was afoot anyway. It was winter, outside and in. The building's unreliable airconditioning, sometimes the source of alarming chemical smells, was now merely blasting out freezing cold air. While other people bundled up, I'd have torn off everything but a cotton teeshirt, rather unnecessarily shouting 'hot flush alert'.

It caused looks of appalled amazement at first. There were more men than women in the immediate vicinity and some were men who grew visibly emotional only over football or cricket scores. They seemed about as liable to share personal revelations as to indulge in cross-dressing. I told them, as I told myself, that I was demystifying menopause. And there was no doubt that the shock value of the announcements wore off rapidly, even if no other woman working for the newspaper had thought to boast at the top of her voice about growing old and withered. When the company installed large electronic bulletin boards, in fact, a colleague, the newspaper's thirty-something High Court correspondent, insisted they were intended to broadcast my hot flush announcements.

But I was tiring of the sensations that provoked them—the six am. sweats, the bizarre compulsion to throw off clothes and blankets in the dead of winter, the odd little stab of anxiety that accompanied the sudden spread of meaningless heat, and the sense that one's body betrayed one with every flush, each as unanticipated as the last, however often they arrived.

The result was that I decided for the first—and most certainly the only—time in my life to resort to Chinese medicine. Reasoning that the Chinese must have been dealing with menopause for thousands of years, I dug out a name and found myself in a beachside suburb in an old house that proved to be a warren of dark rooms. Here and there were cupboards of shelves, filled with big glass bottles of the bits of bark, treestump, herbs and powders that are scraped, pounded, pulverised and boiled according to the herbalist's prescriptions. But they might as well have been part of a stage set, judging by my experience.

The Chinese man who ran the show was square-faced and animated. At ten on a wet, weekday morning, the hangdog doctor with him looked as if he wanted a drink. He shifted from foot to foot as the herbalist looked in my eyes, repeating my diagnosis, hot flushes, and gave my head a little rub. That was that. Looking back, I can scarcely believe that I placed any trust in this process. I am a cautious person. I get enough sleep. I exercise. I swallow vitamins. I never even tried acid when you were supposed to.

In fact I like to think the 1960s left little imprint on me, other than reinforcing the left-liberalism I inherited from my mother. I never had any time for the other legacies of the era, whether grab-bag transcendentalism or faith in iridology and the healing power of crystals, and here I was putting faith in a fellow who rubbed my head and gave me bottles of black pills that tasted like licorice and looked like bat shit.

He said the pills were twelve dollars a bottle. I had to swallow fifteen, three times a day. That made the bat shit more expensive than hormone replacement therapy. The herbalist sold me four bottles. When I returned for more pills, a fortnight later, he asked if I were an actress. It made me feel I was being conned by someone still learning his lines. I didn't go back. But the hot flushes lessened and soon stopped.

out celebrating

The same bottles were sold for about three dollars, in a shop in Chinatown. I bought eight in one fell swoop, and it took a while before I realised that I'd picked up pills with the same name that contained different potions. I thought to check the bottles because something strange was happening to my body. I no sooner finished one period than my breasts started swelling as if I were about to have another. I imagined the scene somewhere in a factory in China, with the workers sprinkling lumps of oestrogen on the bark, or whatever it was. That didn't help my anxieties.

So I went back to Chinatown and wandered in to show the bottles of pills to a Chinese-born pharmacist. 'Oh, you'll never find out what's in these things,' he said cheerfully in a broad Australian accent. It was at that precise moment that I lost all faith in traditional medicine.

My system was a little slow to acknowledge this fact, and in the next few months I was transformed into a kind of menstruating machine. Normally energetic enough to exercise in the mornings, I could barely drag myself out of bed after nine or ten hours of sleep. But there was an upside. With so much oestrogen floating around in my system, I was chirpy as anything.

And it complicated my responses. While asserting that I had rejected hormone replacement therapy because it was a youth serum for middle-aged women into denial, I continued to wonder if HRT patches—or implants—could provide just enough of the hormones to be a mood elevator. A consultation with a hormone specialist saved me from outright hypocrisy. There wasn't any need for me to take HRT, he said, recommending tofu and soya milk for the hot flushes. A question about headaches didn't hold him up long either. If I got headaches after two drinks a night, he said, I should only have one.

In sum, as I approach my fiftieth birthday, I've gone up a size, which seems to mean I'm growing larger and less visible at the same time. I'm reduced to a single Scotch a night; in compensation I ingest large amounts of tofu, a substance that may have almost magical properties but tastes like curds made from cardboard. I shouldn't eat, I can't drink and I don't get laid often enough to make it worth mentioning, and yet the literature—the new genre of books about women over fifty—suggests I must be mad not to be out celebrating.

The usual tone of the exhortations was captured a while back in a newspaper interview with Christine Clarke, the chief executive of the National Menopause Foundation. 'It is a natural thing and it should be a growth experience,' she said, 'something to look forward to . . . ' Yeah, right.

One of the letters from the editors of this book said eight writers had agreed to contribute to an 'anthology of fictions' on the theme of women and ageing. Until then I had imagined contributing a piece of nonfiction—that being more in my usual line—but I couldn't see how to describe the ageing process to which I had so unexpectedly fallen victim without resorting to the very narratives of lost youth and physical deterioration prohibited from the project. And then, as I say, my eye fell on the word 'fictions' and my spirits soared.

Suddenly I understood. While some women were wolfing down oestrogen and reconstructing themselves with everything from silicone injections in the cheeks to tattooed eyebrows, perfecting the ageless baby-doll look about the time they could pick up the age pension, other, more sensible women were merely using fictions. If nothing else it suggested that the human capacity for self delusion was undiminished by ageing.

'Most people don't have major deterioration and it's very variable until well into their eighties,' seventy-something feminist elder Betty Friedan said in an interview several years ago, apparently forgetting that she had no sooner finished her book about the exhilarating business of ageing than she collapsed with a heart condition that required open heart surgery.

But Australians have made their own contributions to the genre. One fell into my hands last year, when I was asked for an article on ageing. This book, 'The Fabulous Fifties', consists of interviews with women who've reached fifty and speak of it with an evangelical fervour that almost seems to suggest they have thrown off their earthly shackles and are free, free, free at last. They describe being sprung not only from the more pressing domestic concerns (now that the children have grown up and flown the coop), but from the pressures of other people's opinions. I wrote at the time that fiftyish feminists who have fought a long battle for recognition only to find themselves marginalised as older women tend to describe ageing as if it were a function of a bad attitude.

When Germaine Greer described it in her book 'The Change', she stumped off in a different direction, slipping into the metaphorical equivalent of a grey cardigan to do the gardening like Boadicea putting in an appearance on 'Burke's Backyard'. Greer insisted that the whole thing was a sort of purification process that let a woman reclaim the self she had been before becoming an instrument of her 'sexual and reproductive destiny'. I fail to see how childless women like myself have been captive to our reproductive destiny in an age of reliable contraception, let alone how we are freer, having reached a time in our lives when our ageing parents need us. But such details no more impinge on the vision of the sunset years as a kind of sunset cruise (with tanned, fit, endlessly busy senior cits, who resemble the soignee couples in magazine ads for retirement funds) than on Greer's vision (with its wavery mysticism and its purified women, somehow hovering above the ground like figures in a Chagall painting). Both are prompted by the same idea that older women can be their essential selves at last.

It happens that they find themselves liberated just when the physical limitations of age are starting to set in—not that anyone much acknowledges the physical limitations.

On the beach this morning, as I lolloped, panting, past the beautiful bodies, I thought with some nostalgia of that time when my parents were as old as I am now and it was possible to sink into middle age without disapproving comment. Back then, getting to be fiftyish meant you were fairly comfortable and your life had settled into an uneventful pattern—a reward for the *sturm und drang* that had preceded it.

Now you are expected to resist that not-quite-imperceptible descent to 'glorious age' (the title feminist author and lawyer Jocelyn Scutt gave her worthy collection of interviews with golden oldies) and to resist with every fibre.

I no sooner mention ageing to one of my contemporaries than she says she's heard of a woman, a grandmother in her eighties, who has just taken up bungee jumping. It seems she takes an angina pill beforehand. My friend couldn't be more impressed but I can't help feeling that it's not what it seems. A woman who swaps crocheting for bungee jumping in her eighties though she suffers from a heart condition sounds to me like a woman who does not want to die a lingering death. Can you blame her?

What's developed in this society as advances in medical science have pushed back mortality at the very time ageing is being metamorphosed into a more acceptable process—at least on paper—is the often unstated corollary that old people ought to be looking after themselves.

The flipside is the real story about ageing, something that will be told over the next few decades, as one government after another decides that the twentieth century phenomenon of retirement is beyond its means in the twenty-first. The population of over sixty-fives will double in the next half-century. Governments contending with diminished employment and a shrinking taxation base will slash age pensions, and reduce access to public health facilities as health insurance companies are limiting coverage for the aged.

There are plenty of other signs that the members of an ageing population will be expected to care for themselves. Professional women may be more in evidence in the workforce but certain kinds of jobs have evaporated so fast that an assembly line worker in her forties or fifties whose factory closes down has little chance of finding work again. Facts like that cannot modify the more pressing political realities and the United States, for one, is *raising* the retirement age.

How convenient, then, to maintain the *fiction* that the aged aren't different enough to merit special treatment. The very word 'ageing' may be held to have unnecessarily negative connotations. In her latest book, North American author Gail Sheehy, the queen of psychobabble, instead calls it 'saging' and goes so far as to ask if the reader will 'progress' or 'decline' with the years.

It's like a religion, isn't it? You take the vow and profess to see the shining light on the hill, even if raising your eyes is a reminder that you're going to have to get glasses, something you've staved off as long as possible because glasses are so distinct a symptom of midlife, along with thinning hair and a thickening middle.

I can't quite see the shining light on the hill but as it happens, I do have a precise image of what it means to have reached the once comfortable age of fifty. I doubt that I'd call it progress, but now that I work with so many people who are decades younger, I can almost get a glimpse of myself as they see me. The image is disconcerting because it's so pale and blurry when I've always thought of myself as vivid. What they see is a middle-aged colleague. Though they're much too polite to say so, they'd no more measure themselves against such a person than they'd measure themselves against a loud, batty aunt. I live in fear that they'll start to humour me, at any moment.

A Midnight Confederacy
JOANNA MURRAY-SMITH

My mother visits me in hospital, bringing no flowers. Her granddaughter lies in a plastic crib, travel-fatigued. I lie in bed, wondering when the dream began: conception? pregnancy? labour?

My mother says all the right things, but there is something absent in the conversation. I wonder if my dead father knows about the baby. I wonder whether agnostics like myself will one day have to pay for capitulation to faith at critical moments. Father, I say to the air grille in the ceiling: Do you know her? Can you see her?

Mama, I say: Is she beautiful? My daughter stares up at her, willing her admiration. I remember when I was a teenager and my mother would say as I went out on a date: You'll pass in a crowd.

We find words to do with birth, to make it reasonable. Isn't she? Isn't she? Isn't she? Inheritances are workshopped in cheerful sing-song; noses, lips, cheekbones are plucked out of her face and tossed around in the air, Picasso faces raining on us. My mother comments on the peony roses my lover brought me, pale dishevelled globes. Pink-white like baby's skin, I say. Silence creeps towards us from the edges of the room. I give out information: She is this. She is that. She is like. She does this.

My mother leaves for the safety of home. She welcomes my adulthood. I notice in her odd cheerfulness that she is pleased by the extra distance between us now that I look towards my own child. My mother is thankful for my efficient body. I deliver her new life. Her face looks like the maquette of a dried river valley, the frightened eyes have the only life left in her face. Yet she has a jauntiness in her step as she backs out of the ward, smiling. It seems as if her mothering is done.

Baby, baby, baby, baby, baby. I sing the word so often, the syllables come apart and begin to sound

a midnight confederacy

foreign. Bay-bee. Have I made it up, this two part sing-song, or is it common parlance? I want to ask the nurse but worry she will think me mad. I hear a voice from the corridor outside my ward say the sound aloud. Baby, baby, baby. That's the word, then.

My baby secures and unseats me, tiny painful creature who seems to have walked out of the sea and flagged me down. Her expression has an orphan pallor, she greets the world unsupervised. Her skin is the colour of pale green olives in the light. When her eyes are closed, the huge mauve circles of her eye sockets look like bruises. I stare at her and ask: Where did you come from?

Around me are other mothers involved in their own introductions. I hear them clucking and cooing behind curtains. I see their slow slippered feet travel past or the quilted belts of dressing gowns trailing. I am in orbit around birth, drifting in my own gravity. The hum of vacuum cleaners and nurse gossip makes a margin of newness between one life over and another begun. Their ordinariness is deceptive.

The hospital smells of organisation, a cold righteous smell to stave off fear. Terror rides the polished corridors. I sense it shimmying along the pipes and down the shutes and through the linoleum tributaries which keep the building alive. The walls reverberate with compressed shivers. Distress is contained within hospital systems, the filling of forms, the making of beds. I counsel myself that I am on the only floor which exudes health.

The death floors, beneath me, seem well-ordered, filled with the steady pulse of electronic monitors and the acceptance of endings. This floor has a frantic grief. Birth spills out, riotous. I see these babies' lives stretching out into poignant narratives. I calculate their life-spans. The dark certainty of disappointments and losses before them, the abandonments, the banal inadequacies of families, the love affairs which will leave them bitter, the march into illness and old age. I know this is not what new mothers should do, but I am sewn into misery.

A new mother arrives from downstairs, her page boy bangs striding this way and that as she waddles from side to side declaring injury, pushing the bridge of her ugly glasses back on her nose. There is something about her plainness that makes me cry. I think it's wonderful that all women have babies, thin, fat, lovely, plain.

a midnight confederacy

She arrives babyless, but carries a small tartan bag, which she props on the bed-covers and unpacks. She places three paperback novels and a crossword dictionary by the bed and a portable cassette player. On the shelf above, she stacks music cassettes and a packet of herbal tea-bags. She places her toilet bag in the cupboard beside the bed and substitutes her personal pillow for the hospital one. Every movement suggests the pleasure of careful planning, as if tidiness is her decadence.

Her baby follows, a tiny pink swaddle wheeled in a clear covered bassinet they use for the delicate arrivals who start life on the floor above. The bassinet is surrounded by doctors and nurses in squeaky shoes. They whisper to each other and to the mother, as if there is something to fear. She responds in little, clipped certainties which exit her small mouth neatly, pushing distress back into its place. Oh yes, she says loudly. Oh, of course.

Later, she gives me a rundown on her blood-pressure problems. Her name is Carol. She has been in the hospital for two months, now thinks herself an expert on it: There isn't anything I don't know! She tells me about the trolley that

something that happens to other people

comes around on Wednesdays and Fridays with the *Women's Weekly* and postage stamps. She says: My baby is Sarah. With an H. She's in that thing because she's cold. She's an early one, but she's doing fine.

Her husband is thin and neat, in army uniform. He exudes the fragile confidence of someone with a crisis under control. He does not seem affected by his wife's dull, cold manner, but holds her hand tenderly and makes tiny jokes. He brings in a half bottle of champagne and they pop it with a minimum of fuss. Tight little laughs tumble over the curtain.

He talks to me with a deliberate easiness while his wife's obstetrician inspects her wounds behind curtains. He prides himself on his gift for pleasant chit-chat. He says how beautiful his daughter is, but we both know she looks hardly human. He says: Girls are easier, that's a good thing. He laughs: No boy will ever be good enough for her! Oh yes, he says, I'm glad she's a girl. There is the pause of uncertainty between us. If she were a boy, she would have been named Bill, for me, he says, and we both hear the edge of impatience in his voice.

Relieved by the scratchy sound of shifting curtains, he says Cheerio and goes back to his wife. Earnest doctor-sounds float towards me. I hear him say to them: One Step at a Time, and then an expert doctor-laugh to keep hysteria at bay.

I listen to Bill and Carol, and watch. Bill stands by the bassinet marvelling at their tiny girl. She tries to cluck and coo, but Carol cannot quite do it. The sounds stick in her throat as if caught in traps. I know how she feels, as if this baby does not belong to her yet.

Baby, baby, baby, who are you and where did you come from? My baby makes me weep all day and night. The nurses' perky intervention makes me crumble. They try to fit my weeping into practical problems with practical solutions. They say: Soon your milk will come. They say: Soon your baby will be able to grasp the nipple. They say: You'll feel better when you're surrounded by your own things.

But I do not weep for my body's apprenticeship. I am filled with opulent misery that will not let go of me. Words fly towards me to make sense of it, but they falter in mid-air, cannot assemble themselves. History. Love. Death. Mother. Husband.

Generations. Pollution. Baby fingers and baby toes and baby nose and baby breath. Transition rattles the floor and ceiling. I've forgotten small words, like breakfast or newspaper. I've forgotten how small I am. I am all life, my baby all future.

Once photos of myself had composed childhood for me, now my daughter is superimposed, colour over black and white. Photographs show me neatly dressed in Peter Pan collars and tartan kilts, smiling as if to prove that in outward ways, I was mothered well. They are my mother's defence exhibits. As I look at my daughter, I wonder what will be mine. I want to ring Mama and say: Help me. She has given birth four times, after all. But my mother and I do not hear each other. We twitter in conversational rhythms, but nothing is said or heard.

It is well known that she abandoned life, gave it away, along with her tea service and family Bible. Long before my father died, she substituted functioning for living, and did not seem to miss it. My mother does not understand my endless faith in feeling, she thinks it a tedious fidelity. She says: Your sensibility is always naked. Why don't you leave it clothed, once in a while?

There was a time my mother used to sing, that's

what my brothers tell me. When the house was full of the optimistic smell of baking and the dreamy lilt of Frank Sinatra songs. She looks like a singer, my mother. She is still pretty despite the lines, high cheekbones in a doll-face, like a thirties movie-star, but her body is tiny and exhausted. My mother stopped singing when I was born. She caught a bug and nearly died. We both stayed in hospital until I was four months old. The nurses called me Pudding, but my mother never used it because she doesn't believe in nick-names.

Time in our house has always been divided into before me and after me, the before me being a time when everything was happy and normal. Something happened to my mother when she was sick, as if the child had flown from her, taking with it her optimism and sweetness, and she was left in the cold grip of adulthood. She fell out with her sisters and brothers and never spoke to them again. She made my father put bars on the windows of our house and took to expressing interest in capital punishment. She saw wickedness in everything.

When my mother visits me in hospital, she holds her handbag under her arm in an iron grip. She will not let her things loose from her.

something that happens to other people

When I was twelve years old and my brothers were fifteen, we moved to a new neighbourhood full of big houses with kidney shaped pools where mothers who wore clingy slack-suits got excited about theme parties. I used to sit on the front step and watch the other kids in the street, billy carting. My mother didn't like us to ask anyone home.

They had no friends, my parents. I know some people tried to befriend them—I remember the discussions over how to decline invitations to school barbecues and neighbours' Christmas drinks—my mother was steadfast. The house always needed cleaning. The children always tired her out. When I was thirteen and in a childish rage, I thrust their Rolodex at them. Look, I screamed. No names. No numbers. Our house was made of surfaces, laminated, carpet-tiled. Even the wood was veneer over chipboard.

In the suburbs, everything was starched and white. Whole lives went past, the details of them never commented on. Eventually my mother stopped leaving the house. She was protected by the anonymity of middle-age, with its own mysteries. Family responsibilities and women's problems and the accepted complexities of wifing—a confident buffer to curiosity or judgement. It just seemed like shyness or busyness and no one made much of a fuss. Apart from us, the only people she spoke to were the delivery boys from the local Safeway, who brought us brown paper bags full of frozen foods.

My father tried to take her out, but in her own quiet way, she seemed to get what she wanted. He clouded her reluctance to leave the house by referring to Your Mother's Devotion to Home and Family, but we weren't fooled. He made a virtue of her madness to keep things neat. He was busy at work and his absence protected him. Home life held itself in check while he was present, waiting for his neatly dressed, optimistic exit. Madness was too theatrical for our family. It belonged to the kind of people who drank wine with dinner.

There was a time when I was fifteen when I tried to woo my mother to soap operas, professing excitement at up-coming weddings, reconciliations and foreseeable tragedies, desperate to cajole feeling from her, if not for the family and its own dramas, then for their small screen imitations.

But my mother was too clever for bad drama. Despite having a life which seemed to my brothers and me dangerously tranquil, she took up tranquillisers instead. Even so easy an addiction could not triumph over her coolness. Even the lovely chemical refuge could not hook her chilly soul. Like all objects in her life which invited fondness, including human, she gave them up.

Once the thought struck me that my mother was not like all mothers, it made its way through me, spiking my blood. I wanted to save her, not knowing that mothers and daughters rarely save each other.

The ward lights go off at 9 o'clock and I am safe in darkness, there is no fortitude to fake. I stare at the baby as she sleeps and wonder at this love that makes everything before seem careful. My heart is anarchic, arteries propelling a concentrated liquid love. I am full up on my baby, she captivates all sense, thought, speculation. When she opens her slate eyes, she looks at me already to be loved.

The midwives are generals and I am a foot-soldier. There are daily triumphs and failings as I try to marshall the forces of my body and my feelings and my will. I report back to them from the field. She will feed. She won't.

Other mothers flip-flop into the nursery in the

a midnight confederacy

night, pink clouds with limbs in wafting nighties, slack bellies preceding them. They sit in the rockers and feed their infants and make small jokes to each other, a midnight confederacy. There is an unspoken charter in the air, that we are a magic sex, all breasts, all wombs, couriers of the future.

I sit with my shoulders bunched equal with my chin, trying to fix my daughter on my breast. Her tiny mouth searches for the nipple, but cannot hold it. Lips and breast slide against each other frantically. Over and over again, the baby and I try to meet each other, stumbling on need. Tears roll out of me quietly, sprinkling my baby. The other mothers make unsentimental comments about their own babies (this big lug) to deflect from trauma in the air.

Carol stumbles into the room in a floral dressing gown, pushing back her glasses, and takes her tiny girl from the night-nurse, remembering to thank her. She sits and feeds her baby from a spoon. We're getting there, we're getting there, she says to the nurse and laughs tightly.

Out of the nursery window, I can see across the city, to the roof of my house, which surprises me by being where it's always been. I imagine streets replotted, neighbourhoods askew. My lover sleeps beneath that roof, curled towards my empty space. If he woke now, he'd see the street-lamp shape of a maniac on the wall, he'd hear the clock tick. He'd see the blue vase on the tallboy with the pale pink proteas and my red linen coat slung over the wicker chair. He'd hear the fridge hum and the first doves fuck in the courtyard.

When I go home, there will be another heart inside that house, pumping away inside a papery chest. I watch my roof, as if it is about to slink away in the darkness. I left that house only days ago, but it belongs to history. I wonder whether my lover will catch up to me, or if we will always sleep in different places now. Will he wake with me to hear the puff-puff baby breath? Will he walk barefoot across floor-boards, to touch her cool cheek, to remind the little body of its occupation?

The mid-wife asks me what my daughter's up to: Is she taking it? Is she sleeping? I look down at my baby and wonder who it is, this person I am now the only expert on.

Mama, Mama, Mama. I've felt so distant from her for so long, I've forgotten the terror I used to feel at our connection. How when we shared a house I would watch her sleep and wonder how much of her I carried in me, despite my cultivated strangeness. And how our faces were built as perfect replicas, so that old photographs of her appear to be me, surrounded by the muted colours and studio stillness of another era.

Now, there is the third. She lies before me, and underneath my lover's smudged features, the hasty expressions of my mother and me cross like clouds.

In the morning, I watch Carol while I fill in the daily menu. I tick boxes for lemon delicious pudding and study her while she does the crossword, consulting the crossword dictionary. She asks me to answer her phone if it rings while she's in the shower. She thanks me. She asks me questions about my daughter with pleasant disinterest. She has heard me weeping and does not want to catch it.

During the day I hear her call her husband at the army base. She insists they find him. She sounds very sensible when she speaks to him, detailing Sarah's attempts to feed. She says: We can't work miracles overnight. She says: It's a waiting game, that's all. She says dully: There's no point getting worked up about it.

She speaks to her mother in New Zealand. Her flat responses sound as if she's talking to an envious colleague. She speaks so coolly, the words shrivel in the air. She has Bill's eyes and my nose. If you call between six and ten on a Sunday, it's half price.

When her sister rings, she thanks her for the lovely flowers. She describes them in detail, because it's thoughtful to let her know whether the florist overcharged or not.

Carol does not look at her baby. She turns pages of her book and buffs her nails. She sticks headphones on her ears and rewinds and fast-forwards, staring at the pages of her important paperback. I hear the jaunty scratches of pop songs trapped inside metal. But over the next day, she casts little glances into the bassinet, and by Thursday, stands beside it, looking in blankly.

Later, we eat from our trays silently. When the drinks trolley comes around, she calls the trolley maid by name. She says: Diane, could I get an extra milk-shake please? She drinks one with dinner and saves one for later, keeping the little paper ceiling over it. Because the other bed in the room is empty, the silence volleys between us conspicuously.

Finally, she says to me, Sarah should come out of there tomorrow. I want to get home soon as possible, get settled into the new life.

I do not want to leave the hospital today or tomorrow or ever. I do not want to take my daughter home to choking meals or falling stairs or drowning baths. I do not want to be alone with her in case she comes apart like a doll.

When breath stops, in fleeting ordinary moments, how can I be sure to hear her over the sounds of cars, of birds, of dreams?

In the night I suffocate myself in the cold linen, protecting Carol from my terror-cries. I cannot believe that I belong to the mothers, how childhood has capsized on birth.

What did I see, those years ago, when I looked out of my cot at my mother? A woman with a face so white, it seemed translucent, a woman expecting death? How did she look at me, swaddled in hospital blankets, demanding life? Once my mother lay in this ward, a ward like this one. And watched her future cross my face.

In the house, alone at night, she must camouflage her losses to stop them from killing her. Perhaps she had always dismissed love as something too precious to own, and taken my father into her life as someone neither better than her nor beneath her, but rather equal to her own vacancy. He provided no contrast, and that was important to a woman for whom conspicuousness was terror.

Had she loved him once, or were my brothers and I the dutiful result of a dutiful surrendering? In our house, there was no talk of love. Our house shouted its preference for the present. It busied itself in the tiny moments of every day, never looking forward or backward from the calendar date on my father's unused desk. Nostalgia was unknown to us, too close to love.

I wonder if I am so ill-equipped for the simple getting on with things, because of my mother's dedication to it. A life of getting on with things, of ironing what needs to be ironed and folding what needs to be folded, of reducing birth and marriage and even death to lists of practical steps, of sandwiches made and bank accounts altered. A life of closing down the call to joy, and even to grief, because they cause equal trouble.

I am a convert to symbolism, regret, love, the passing of time, the canonisation of moments. I have a thousand boxes at home with keepsakes, embalming affections that were never really worthy. I am a collection of reactions and inheritances, every one a vigilant rebellion. I am so steadfast in not being my mother, I am compelled by the nervousness that is the heart of her.

My lover visits me and stares at his daughter. He never asked for this, but now that he holds her he shows no loyalty to ancient expectations. He seems to see all three of us as innocents who have woken up suddenly in a complex place.

I look at myself in the mirror and see my face ravaged by the shock of love. Lines in my forehead, sun-made, baby-made. Hazy fragments of my mother's face worry their way over me, insinuating credit. I think how young we were those months ago when we sent her tiny impulse hurtling towards this debut. Our overturning hearts make us weep together. We talk about baby furniture, turning our minds into nurseries, hoping the images of cots and change-tables will anchor our feelings to the floor.

In the afternoon I lift my baby from cot to bed and lie with her cradled in my arm. I have not slept for four days or nights, in case she disappears from me. I stare at the skinny limbs that used to push

something that happens to other people

my stretched skin upwards, as if she was pounding to come out.

Later, Carol says: Your husband seems thrilled! I say: So does yours! We are trying desperately to fight the knowledge creeping into the room and fixing itself to things that we don't like each other. We laugh about husbands in a knowing sort of way, as if they are the real children, hoping to ally ourselves. She offers me her orange. I offer her my apple. We make a big song and dance about this, but it's useless.

In the night, my baby sleeps in the nursery so that I can close my eyes. I fall into cavernous space. Babies fly in and out of frame, like seagulls. I am aware that I have lost consciousness and I am erotically wrapped in sleep.

And then there is the sound of Carol. At first, a sound of neutral business, of metal wheels and curtains in the dark. Buzzers, shouts, the flat plastic sound of nurse shoes skipping down corridor. Bed lights switch on tight pockets of light. Carol making noises, hard little gasps, phrases lifting into air then falling, nurses talking over-quickly, staving something off. The jangling sounds of the unexpected falling over us, over the heaviness of beds and trays and water jugs, of clipboards on the ends of beds and visitors' chairs.

The lights go on. My watch says it's ten to four. Carol is supported by two nurses, who help her walk past my bed and out into the corridor. Her gasps shake the stillness out of the night. Sarah's bassinet is missing. I lie, waiting.

The nurse brings me my baby for feeding. I lay her by my side, her tiny hand caressing the curve of breast, mouth ready. The nurse sits beside me, ready to help attach her. I ask her where Carol has gone. She says to me: Carol's little girl is very ill.

Sarah and my baby merge into a single child, hovering on the outskirts of death.

In the morning, Carol is back in bed, doped up to keep her fear lethargic. She sleeps for hours, Bill beside her. The curtains are drawn, but I can hear the even relayed breaths, first hers, then his. By evening, Bill leaves because there is nowhere for him to sleep. I try to speak. He nods.

I want to speak with Carol, but the anticipation chokes me. She stays in bed and reads her book and listens to her cassettes. She goes for long walks, returns to talk in whispers to the hospital counsellor, a woman with a tiny silver cross around

something that happens to other people

her fat neck. I cannot speak of her baby, who disappeared in the night. The nurse tells me Sarah is on the floor beneath, struggling to live.

I walk the corridors, pushing my daughter in front of me, sleeping a newborn's weighty sleep. I recognise my mother in my nervous step, the bottled-up panic, the paranoia about other people, who cannot be confided in. I smell of disinfectant on stainless steel. Perhaps my feeling is all theatre and underneath, I am my mother as certainly as she is hers.

In the morning, I pack my things and throw away the shrivelled roses. I wait for the doctor to weigh my baby in the nursery and then I bathe and dress her in the clothes I bought for her. When I walk back to the ward, I find my mother talking to Carol and stumble backwards out of the room. I stand in the corridor, beside my daughter's cot.

She's a fighter, I hear my mother say, and her words stream out of her, moving in circles like a continuous calming prayer. You have faith in her. You have faith in the doctors. She's a darling little girl and she's fighting very hard.

I hear tiny blurred noises from Carol and look around the corner at them. My mother sits beside her, leaning forward, her face only inches away from Carol, whose head rests back on her pillow. I don't remember ever being that close to my mother. I wonder what she looks like that close.

My mother's voice sings with sorrow, her words are gifts to Carol. All the sweetness sits between them, some feminine and knowing history. I am startled to see Carol's hand move to my mother's, resting on the blanket, and brush it. Silence then, for maybe a minute. And then my mother's brittle arms reaching around Carol's bulky body, holding her, and the sound of two women weeping.

The Jarrah Thieves
ELIZABETH JOLLEY

High up on the edge of a dilapidated wooden verandah overlooking a shallow ravine of restless eucalyptus and wandoo trees a young man, temporarily expelled from his university, sat opposite his old aunt watching her eat breakfast with an appetite he was unable to share. She was so thin that when she swallowed he could see the food going down her throat. And all the time she talked in an economical but vivid English which was sometimes only understandable to those who knew her very well. She spoke a great many languages but had never taken the trouble to learn one of them properly.

'Back home in Vienna,' she swallowed, apparently with difficulty, a crust of her own home-made bread, 'back home, you know, you know Manfred, you would spend some time away in the mountains. Here in this country we have no mountains but my place here is a thousand feet over the sea level so breathe while you are here,' she continued. 'More coffee? Drink if eat you cannot, is good, dandelion coffee. I grind myself!' But after his sleepless night in her big empty wooden house he had a bad headache. He had the headache before he came, it was from the noise and the wind and the jokes with his fellow students at the medical school dinner the night before.

'Did you not feel your ears crackle when you came up?' she asked. 'Mine always! even after all these years. Come along,' she urged, 'another cup will make you well.'

'No thanks Aunty.'

She shrugged her thin shoulders and helped herself.

The wind in the perpetually swaying tree tops was like an endless lullaby in the rocking cradles of branches and leaves. Morning, noon and night, the light and shade and the colours and the outlines of these trees were changing all the time. At all times of the day and at night there was something different about them to notice and enjoy.

He tried to take his aunt's advice: a heron flew alone emerging from time to time between the trees, looking for food. Manfred breathed in the air, it was fragrant with fried eggs and the frail smoke from stumps and tree roots and bits of blackboy burning. And every now and then the heavy scent of fermenting grapes and mulberries came up to them on an extra breath of wind from the neglected, overgrown terraces immediately below the verandah of the house.

From the other side of the valley came a dull rumbling sound and a log-carrying trailer with a blue and white cabin in front went by. The old woman shaded her eyes with one hand, she nodded with approval as the truck passed an open space where a dead tree held up its great antlers into the middle distance between the earth and the sky.

'Quick!' she said to Manfred, 'count the chains, my eyes are not what they used to be, there should be four chains.' The young man looked with obedience, the huge logs were loaded with their glowing cut ends facing outwards, he was not sure where the chains should be.

'One at either end and two in the middle,' screamed his aunt over the noise of the laden vehicle, she was straining across the rail of the verandah trying to see.

'It's all right,' she calmed down, 'I saw them!' The noise gradually became fainter as the truck continued on its headlong journey to the great black smoky scar in the countryside some five miles further on where pig iron was made. The old lady besides owning the several acres of orchards and vineyards, mostly planted by herself years ago when she had come with her father as a girl to start a new life in another country, also owned some miles of timber, a great jarrah forest acquired with some foresight years ago when the virgin land was being sold, by present day standards, very cheaply. She was selling timber to the foundry.

'Fortunately for me,' she explained to her nephew, 'they are still old-fashioned enough to fire their furnaces with wood. It is a black place, before you go you must see this great black sore we have, but for me, thanking God, it is there!'

There were five log-hauling trucks and, before leaving the verandah, his aunt remained at the rail till all of them had gone by. The noise of their

the jarrah thieves

rumbling and the bright colours of the cabins wherein the drivers sat hidden and his aunt screaming over the heavy traffic; 'Count the chains!' and 'See! Number three is wrongly loaded!' created a diversion, a considerable disturbance in the quiet tranquillity of the little valley.

'Tonight I shall make your dinner myself,' she promised, looking at him fondly. He was her only relative, his father, her younger brother, had died some years ago and as she had never liked her brother's wife, she did not consider her to be a relation. 'Tonight I make a soup for you out of my own head. But first we make little outink to the jarrah forest. I have work for you there. Students are always penniless, is that not so, I give you some work,' she said, 'and then I pay you something!'

They were walking to and fro on the terraces. Every now and then his aunt interrupted her talk with him to scream orders to the two plump girls who kept house for her and who were supposed to do mysterious things to the vines and the fruit trees at the right times.

'They are lazy girls,' she explained to him. 'That is why I have to shout at them all the time.' She had spent most of her life wielding a pick and shovel, digging holes and carting soil and planting trees, and she had spent hours bent in half, weeding or putting potatoes in the earth, muttering prayers and curses to the rain and the wind and the sun and the frost. Everyone who did not do these things all the time was lazy, this was not so much her opinion but rather because of her accustomed way of life.

'Apricots, plomms, nectarines, peaches, almonds, apples,' his aunt showed him the trees. They were all old like she was and their insides were eaten away by white ants; she broke a small branch to show him.

'But we have the fruit all the same,' she said striding just a few feet ahead of her nephew. She waved her arm to the bottom paddock. 'Down there are pear trees and quince. Do you like quince jelly? I have made! So you shall try!' She poked her stick into some scuffed-up leaves where a goanna, seeking privacy to change his skin, lay unblinking as if dead.

'Strange creatures! We can never know how old they are,' she muttered as if half to herself. Manfred supposed she talked to herself a great deal as she spent all her time alone except when she was ordering the people who worked for her about their business. Her nephew's visit pleased her very much and she did not question why, after all this time, he had come to stay with her when she had not seen him since he was a little boy. He scarcely remembered the place though he had been there years ago with his father. Any uneasiness he felt on the way there (he had been fortunate to get a lift) about his welcome was quickly lost, his aunt had been delighted when he came. They paused beyond the pear orchard by a narrow rotten bridge. The creek, full with its first flow of water after the long hot dry summer, looked stagnant and dirty.

'Is not rain yet,' his aunt explained. 'Is seepage water soaking through, now that it is not so hot, water is not evaporated from the earth, will look clearer later on. Your father,' she continued, 'made this bridge. I bring him up when he was little boy and then he left to go on a life of his own,' she sighed. 'You played here too, you know.'

'Did I?' Manfred tried the bridge with his weight, it sank and water oozed between and over the old railway sleepers from which it was made. The butter-like banks of the creek were slippery and quite steep.

'Careful!' his aunt warned. 'You can repair later,' in her voice was the promise of a treat.

To go to the jarrah forest which was some miles away she drove an old car. She followed the reploughed fire breaks through the bush, as they cut down the distance and, since no one else drove there, she had these tracks to herself and did not have to concern herself at all with the ethics and rules of driving.

'Sometimes I bog myself down,' she said and threw a spade and an old coat and some sacks into the back of her car. 'They make open the old fire breaks,' she complained. 'And this makes the ground too soft for my car.'

It was like turning over a page in a picture book so quickly did the scrub of blackboys, hakea and sheoaks change into the jarrah forest. First they went through a part from which all the big old trees had been removed. Here a slender forest of secondary growth had grown up, the tall thin trees close together crowded out the sun and the fire break was, as his aunt said, very soft. The car only just went through. They came out at last on to a hard wide gravel track; below them stretching for miles was the forest of big old trees.

'Here my trucks come up,' his aunt said and she drove on down to overlook an area which was being cleared. A kind of devastation of earth and tree moving and cutting and burning lay before them. Huge trees with dark bleeding bark, the colour wrapped round their massive trunks by fire and by the sun, lay about the clearing. All round fires were smouldering, sometimes flames leapt up here and there and men in helmets were going about in this apparent disorder, working with machinery, pushing down the trees, heaving them about, cutting them up and loading the trailers.

The air was so clear that the blue smoke hung in patches as if put there for decoration, and the great noise of the work came up to them as if from some far away place. The old lady looked down with approval on the scene.

'Go on down to them,' she said to her nephew. 'The old man in the white hat is the foreman, tell him I have sent you to work, tell him to teach you something. You can get home on the last run to the foundry. Ask for to be put off on the road at the foot of my place. Mind the bridge!' She turned the car and stuck her head out of the window, her shoulder length grey hair framing her thin face.

'Josst listen to the music of the chain-saws! What an invention!'

The magic of the jarrah forest seemed to be on all sides of him as he walked down. In this new place it seemed as if the days before this one had never been or as if they had belonged to someone else's life. He longed to go on walking and walking, away from the workmen, as if he might all at once emerge in some hitherto unknown and wonderful world.

'These lady tutors they insist on full-time permanent posts,' his professor complained. He was so absorbed in his problems of administration he hardly looked up from the papers on his desk to glance at Manfred as he diffidently entered the room. 'And then, when they get them,' he went on, 'they aren't satisfied, they weep even, here in my room, see I even have tissues for them, because they say I am unfair, they say they can't get here to give nine o'clock lectures and they can't stay for tutorials and demonstrations after four o'clock in the afternoon because they have domestic duties and baby-sitting problems.' Manfred stood just inside the door while the older man continued his monologue. 'Why can't they themselves stay with their babies and save me from all this worry, I don't understand. Why do they have babies at all?' He looked up suddenly at Manfred as if to say, 'Why are you intruding upon my private worries?' Instead he said, 'So you have refused to register for national service,' knowing immediately, as is the way with an academic mind, how to dispose of the fringes of untidy thought and unnecessary words. 'You refuse yet you know you would be exempt for the present. And you are accused of writing an obscene article in our journal. I have seen the article, I am not disposed to discuss it, it has merit. If you offend, you alienate yourself and you do not make contact, you could write what you have written without the use of those certain words. Secondly, if you want to protest for peace then do it in peace. You burnt your cards and resisted arrest. But what is the use, I am not accusing you. All I say is violence will not get rid of violence. Temporarily I gather you are dismissed. I shall do what I can on your behalf. Do not expect too much from me or too little. At all events,' here he gave his smile which he kept for the young men in the middle of their medical studies, 'I shall keep you out of gaol. I want rather to see you in the operating theatre!'

All this now seemed to belong to another time and place, to another person even; as he walked down it seemed as if he had always been with his aunt, in her house, with her strange mixture of the frugal with a certain luxury of well-being, even her dandelion coffee was not so bad. He had come to her rather than go home to his mother.

'How can you do this to me?' was her phrase always and he felt he couldn't explain that he wasn't doing anything to her, only to himself. If his thoughts and actions could affect the world then he would stick to what he felt were the best thoughts and actions he had to offer, even if some part of the world he had to be in found him wrong or obscene. As he walked, it comforted him to think that if the University refused to take him back he could, after all, perhaps stay on with his aunt. Her meals were a great comfort, or would be when he had thrown off the effects of the students' party, and there was too the great comfort and security in property.

That night his professor was addressing the Thoracic Society at a dinner. How far away that dinner seemed and the professor himself in his half-lensed gold-rimmed glasses. Mahler, his favourite composer wore spectacles like them. Mahler knew forests and the irresponsible frivolous rustling of leaves and the wonder and praise one could feel about the sight of a tree together with the great sadness and melancholy and the pain of the earth. It was strange that one could know, in a way, more about a man who had written music years ago than about a man one had spoken to and listened to almost daily for the whole of the preclinical course in Medicine.

The smell of the freshly-cut timber, and the hot smell of the chain-saws came sharply to him. It was suddenly quiet in the clearing. Manfred, deep in his thoughts, walking down through the trees, had not seen the men gather behind one of the little huts they had there. For a moment he thought they had seen him coming and did not want him and had hidden to discuss what was to be done. Then he thought that perhaps there had been an accident. He hoped fervently that no one had had an accident, for though he knew the names of all the bones and systems in the body and had already learned a great many of the things that could go wrong either by accident or by disease or by old age, he was not yet able to fit the frail pages of his books and the words of his teachers to the flesh and blood and the feelings of a human being. He felt quite unequal to seeing the distress and pain of a man trapped under a tree, and was quite sure he would not know what to do in any circumstances if someone should shout, 'Is there a doctor here?' 'A junior nurse in a hospital would know more than I do if someone was hurt,' he thought, and standing alone at the edge of the clearing in the jarrah forest he felt afraid.

'There's nothing in the world like a really good woman,' a voice came out into the stillness from behind the hut.

'True,' another voice helped the story teller. 'Very true.' Manfred stayed at the side of the shed as the first man went on talking.

'At school I sat behind a girl. I never saw her face much, always her shoulders,' the narrator paused to drink noisily from a tin cup, he lit a cigarette. 'I used to look over her shoulder and peer at her work, such beautiful neat handwriting, I wanted to copy it and write as well, and I tried to see her face but she never turned around.' The men were eating and drinking and smoking, some sitting on the ground, some on cut logs and others standing, they made a pattern of rest and ease as they took both.

'And then later, much later, I saw her again, only the back of her, she was working at a big table in a bakery and I asked her name but it meant nothing to me as you'll never believe how stupid I was. I never knew the name of the girl in front of me at school! I found it was the same girl. She used to get cross with the man who drove the bread cart. He whipped the horse so much and once she came out and saw all the strokes of the whip on the horse and she shouted so much that I, yes men it was me! I, fool that I was! I never went back there. As I didn't go the next day to drive the bread cart,' his voice deepened and broke very slightly in the silence, 'she drove the horse and the bread cart herself. It was only half an hour's drive but she had been so hot in the bakehouse and she went without her jacket and she caught a chill and died quite quickly in terrible pain, you know, what do you call it? Pleurisy. Such a lovely girl and only quite young.' A long silence followed the woodman's story and Manfred still waited beside the hut, not liking to intrude.

'I had a dog,' another voice broke in to lighten the weight which had settled on them.

'Yes tell us,' another voice helped the new story teller.

'Well this dog was so intelligent he used to bite the fleas off himself and lay them on the bed,' there was a burst of laughter interrupting the story.

'How could a dog lay a flea?' came from someone.

'But no,' the first voice continued, 'he used to lay them on the bed and count them!' More laughter.

'Ah. Women!' another voice sighed in a foreign accent. 'I have seen the glow of youth and the beauty of being in love and the sweet prettiness of young motherhood changed overnight into weariness and perpetual discontent!'

'Talking about fleas,' said yet another voice, 'I had a dog who had fleas that bad he was quite mad with them. And he went up to a sheep and said beg pardon let me have a bit of your wool. The sheep took no notice, perhaps she was deaf, I don't know, but the dog took a tuft of her wool and holding it between his teeth he jumped in the creek. As you know fleas can't stand cold water, the dog sank in the water so that just the bit of sheep's wool was sticking out and when all the fleas had climbed on to the bit of wool he let it go and came out of that creek without a flea on him.' A burst of laughing followed this.

'That's an old story, I heard that one before or else I read it somewhere.'

'What! *you* read something! That's a story in itself!'

'Anyway I never heard of a dog being able to talk, let alone ask a sheep for anything,' said someone in tones obviously meant to smooth things over. 'Or a deaf sheep, who ever could know if a sheep was deaf or not! Well men! Time for work!'

Manfred came round the hut and the old man in the white helmet set him to sharpening a saw at once, showing him how to wedge the blade in a specially-prepared crack in a log, how to hold the file and then the delicate but firm correct movement of the file. And once more the noise and activity and the dust filled the clearing. The light of the day was coloured with the red glow of the newly-cut wood and the men could not speak to each other because of the noise of the axes and the chain-saws and the earth and tree moving machines. One by one the trailers with the different brightly-coloured cabins came back to be reloaded ready for the headlong rumbling journey to the foundry where the furnaces were hungry for the wood. And back at home Manfred's aunt was busy with her accounts and the profits from the cutting down and selling of the timber which had taken such years to grow and was her good fortune to possess. She was bothered with her accounts, there was a mistake somewhere and never before had she made mistakes and now there was a regular one. She turned back the pages and went through the lists of figures over and over again. Adding up and subtracting, even if it was wrong, gave her pleasure.

All day Manfred worked in the jarrah forest and all day he tried to fit to the different faces the various stories that were told. The stories seemed in themselves to have no significance except that they filled the silence with a kind of philosophical brotherly entertainment when all the machines were quiet.

And yet there was meaning in the stories for they

belonged to human beings and the things they thought about, all the things that worried or pleased them. He almost told them.

'I know a young man who punched three policemen and went to hide with his aunt,' but he didn't know the men at all, not like they knew each other. They were kind enough to him, considerate even, the foreman, the old one in the white helmet, sat beside him at noon and offered him bread and olives and a piece of bacon fat from his own hessian bag. But he was too shy to tell his story, he would not have known how to receive their disbelief or their laughter or their boredom or their admiration. They could all take these things from one another. So he worked and looked on.

It was a long day, they worked till dusk, the fires glowed all round them burning the twigs and leaves, they seemed at times to be in a wide circle of fires. He was warm all through his body from the work and from being in the fresh air.

He was to ride home in one of the log-hauling trucks, he noticed it had been loaded with smaller logs, all of them cut and split unlike the logs chained on to the other trailers but he was too tired to ask why this was. The trucks set off up the wide gravel track, their engines whining and groaning in low gear. When they reached the top the foreman in the white helmet stood there at the edge of a dark clump of trees and stopped every truck in turn to allow the truck in front plenty of time to start off down the hill on the headlong rumbling journey to the foundry.

When he woke up he was cold and stiff, still in the cabin of the truck; someone had thrown some sacks over him. The driver was nowhere to be seen. The morning was damp and the sun was coming through the trees dispersing the mist in long white fraying ribbons. Cocks were crowing and he looked out and saw he was in a strange place where he had never been before. The truck was parked close up beside the smallest cottage he had ever seen. It was like a nut, brown and uneven, made from old wood and iron and the chimney pipe was rusted and fastened by wires to the edges of the sloping roof. A woman in a blue overall came out and was at once surrounded by hens, and a bit later on seven geese came in a long line from the bottom of the meadow below the little nut of a cottage. All round, in among some old almond trees, were heaps of split jarrah logs, small mountains of logs, one after the other, some of the heaps were as big as the cottage. An axe lay beside a chopping block and a large basket was fixed to a spring balance which hung from the branch of a fig tree in the front part of the yard. There were axe heads and broken handles and discarded toys and two long lines of washing, mostly rags, the things worn by children when they have not enough clothes to wear.

Stiffly Manfred climbed down from the cabin and the woman asked him, 'Will you stop for some tea and porridge?' The truck driver came slowly from the cottage.

'I'll just unload,' he muttered and climbed back into the cabin after unfastening the chains. The noise of the wood falling brought several sleepy children tumbling from the cottage. The wood roared from the tipped-up trailer into a great heap.

'More wood, more wood,' they chanted. The woman tried to send them off but they wanted to hug the driver and Manfred who was quite bewildered. 'You'll stop for tea?' the woman asked again. But the driver refused in quite a surly tone saying they had not time and must go at once.

The sun came up quickly and lit up the far away

tops of the trees in the jarrah forest as they drove towards it.

'She keeps a wood yard,' the truck driver explained reluctantly to Manfred. 'She sells the wood to the people in the township just down the road from where her place is, they come to her for it, it is her living. She lost her husband ten years ago, a tree fell on him, he was deaf, he couldn't hear us shouting at him, he was using the axe, he was the best axe we had.'

'But the children are all little ones,' Manfred began.

'Yes,' the other agreed, 'but it so often happens that way to a woman on her own if she has a kind heart,' he shrugged. The truck was coming near to the orchards.

'I should 'ave put you off here last night but you were that sound asleep!'

'Thank you all the same.' Manfred climbed down from the cabin and ran through the sweet fragrance of the summer as it lingered on in the withered grass. The season was changing to autumn.

The pear trees, covered in yellow leaves, were like little silent watchmen in yellow oilskins. The sun had not reached them yet as they were down on the mud flats near the creek. Manfred trod lightly over the old bridge and almost flew up the rough terraces to tell his aunt how the men were cheating her.

It was quite clear that every night a load of wood went to the lonely little cottage full of children, and all the time his aunt thought she was selling that wood to the foundry. He would be able to tell her the truth and prevent her from losing more money.

'Where are you Aunt?' he called, very much out of breath with running.

His aunt was kneeling on the verandah with her long skirts pinned up, she was oiling the boards with linseed oil and turpentine. The smell reminded him for a moment of the games pavilion at school. He almost felt like a small boy about to tell tales, and the sharp smell of the oily mixture brought back vividly the bitter loneliness of the long days and eternal afternoons, of the desolation of homesickness and of hating school and the cloakrooms and the dormitories and the games pavilion where all the other boys always seemed to get on so well with one another. It was better to be with his aunt; the girls, laughing about something between themselves, were putting the breakfast on the table. The red coffee pot looked splendid, it seemed to be the most beautiful thing he had seen.

He thought he would tell his aunt about the stolen wood later on, he felt he must tell her but just now he was so hungry.

Later she was by the verandah rail waiting for the first of the trucks to come by. There was no chance to tell her what he had discovered.

'Always look at a person's hands,' she said to her nephew. 'From their appearance and the way he holds them and what he does with them, in looking at a person's hands,' she said, 'you will learn much about the person. Never take anyone's hands for granted,' she said and then her talk was lost as one of her trailers marked *Martha Dobsova's Jarrah Mills* was rumbling and about to pass the gap where the dead tree implored the pale sky for something with its great antlers which were, this morning, like gaunt arms stretched up.

'Look at the chains!' she screamed above the noise but Manfred was looking at his aunt's hands, they were rough, the knuckles were enlarged with hard work and the skin, though shining with oil just then, was thin like burnt paper and mottled brown with the kind of patches old people have on their hands. Her hands were strong and they were also very kind.

Every day he went to work in the jarrah forest. He even stayed there with the men in one of the little huts and took his turn working at night with them. They remained friendly with a quiet acceptance of him though he was not one of them. Often he went in the specially-loaded truck, the one with the small split logs, to the little nut cottage and listened to the children laughing and shouting over the deafening roar of the logs being unloaded. He kept thinking he must tell his aunt of the robbery or else tell the men they shouldn't steal the wood but he couldn't bring himself to do either, and often he paused at his work in indecision and despised himself. He had never felt like this before. He was always studying and learning and reading, he enjoyed the company of his fellow students but had no close friend. He took part in the moratorium marches against the war because he really believed all war to be wrong. He was overcome with a surprise so deep that it was a pain when he lost his temper and swung his fists at the policeman. It was almost as though he was watching an unknown person do these things and his own voice was unrecognisable to him, the owner of it. It was a kind of shocked state of mind which made him love the jarrah forest and caused him to find the thing he had discovered so difficult and unpleasant just when he was seeking to heal himself.

One day he told his story to the men in the forest '. . . you see I feel that the war is senseless . . .' He felt his voice was not like theirs, his education and the things he hoped to do might not be acceptable to them and again, as at the beginning, he felt afraid. His story was not like theirs except that to him it had the same core of human predicament.

'Ah well!' they said and stood around and made their usual comments, taking their rest as they needed it.

'Who can tell what is best for a man to do.'

'It's easy enough to tell a man what he ought to do but whether it's right or not is another matter.'

'Who can know how a man should be, he can only feel what he feels he is and is the best he can be.'

'True.'

'Too right!' They all shifted their muscular sunburnt bodies a little. Compared with them Manfred seemed to have no body at all, but no one had ever seemed to notice. Some of the men wore thin gold chains around their necks, some had little discs on them and others a golden cross. He felt envious of the wearing of these gold chains, they gave the men an air of distinction as if they had been given a secret blessing; their distinction was the more distinguished as they paid no attention to the chains and took for granted the precious thing they possessed.

'Talking about fleas, have you ever heard of the two fleas who thought they would keep a boarding house . . .?'

'Who ever heard of fleas thinking, let alone thinking of keeping a boarding house,' the old man stirred himself, he often looked as if he was asleep in the middle of them. 'Time for work! Come on, get going!'

And again, as all the other times before, the clearing was busy with work. Fires blazed and smouldered by turns, and the noise of the machinery and the chain-saws made a kind of symphony together with the straining of the heavy chains pulling on the great logs and the whine of the trailers slowly crawling up the slope in slow gear.

Of course he couldn't tell them about the article he had written: his first appearance in print had pleased him very much. But now his subject and his choice of words seemed so far away from this life in the jarrah forest, though what he had written concerned them and the woman in the nut of a cottage full of little children. But when he thought of the woman teaching in the university and wanting someone to look after her baby and this other woman in the little hut seeking nothing more than enough food and a few clothes for her children, he began in his mind comparisons of problems. And when he went to the cottage again and saw the woman and the children playing hide and seek among the mountains of stolen wood, he realised he had tried to write about something which was as yet entirely beyond him. How small he felt among these great trees.

On the day he returned to his aunt's house she was surrounded by calico sacks, they looked like little pillows marked with her name *Dobsova*.

'Seed,' she said. 'Blue lupin, Yarloop clover, Wimmera rye grass and strawberry clover.'

It was a poem of seeds; she checked the bags with a list she had in her strong old hand.

'If I can get the hoe going I'm going to sow the bottom paddock,' she explained, 'and on the terraces something too, holds the earth, stops the topsoil from washing away.' She screamed for the girls to bring breakfast.

Manfred after his few days in the forest felt he had to tell his aunt about the stealing of the wood. He did not really want to tell her because it would mean the men concerned would be sacked and the woman and the little children would lose the only living they had.

'Always I have troubles with the hoe,' his aunt said. 'Thanking God you are here! You can pull the rope to start it, I am too old!'

Here she was interrupted by the two girls running onto the verandah without the plates and cups they were expected to bring.

'Bassett's place is afire!' they came crying, 'fire at Bassett's!'

'The fools! Blockheads! They always every year do this!' his aunt rose up tall among the little pillows of seeds. 'Always it is the same the day for forbidding fires is past,' she said. 'But blockheads! they are so stupid, they light to burn off but we have had no rain, it is still not safe to burn just because it is the end of the forbidden time! Every year they do this silly thing!'

She strode across the verandah.

'Get my sacks and wet them,' she told the girls. 'And be quick!' They all went out to her car as quickly as they could.

There was about the morning a strangeness. In the distance the jarrah forest looked quite different as if dusk had come too soon: long curtains of quiet grey smoke were being drawn by ghost hands between the trees. The sky was orange behind a lattice of the same grey smoke. Some trees looked bigger than they really were while others were completely wrapped in smoke.

'Is the forest on fire?' Manfred asked anxiously, he was thinking about the men in the clearing in the heart of it. It was such a short time since he had leapt from the cabin of the truck to run up to his aunt's house.

'Not yet, it is only Bassett's place. Is only ten acres but the tenants are feckless, always no job, always neglect! That place is nothing to me, I go only to save my place, my sheds are that side and my best fruit trees. I won't have my place burned by their stupidity!'

It was some days before he could speak to his aunt, she was restless watching the sky waiting for rain clouds. She kept leaning over the verandah rail, the house behind her quietly waiting too for the rain. She wanted to sow her lower paddock.

'The clouds come,' she complained. 'And always just here they divide and one dark cloud goes over to one side and the other cloud beeg with rain, it goes over to the other side. Always is like this!' And she paced over the rough boards. 'Someone else gets my rain!'

The two girls were sulky and one looked as if she had been weeping. Manfred was on the point of telling his aunt.

'What is wrong with them?' he asked, rather than say what was on his mind. His aunt took her attention from the sky.

'Oh, they are sulking a bit,' she said. 'We are a houseful of women. They expected to be seduced while a young man stay in the house. They are disappointed that is all, they will get over it!'

His aunt was so far from thinking of the men in the jarrah forest, she peered at the trailers as they passed her house and sometimes exclaimed half-heartedly, 'Number three is loaded badly,' but she was busy with the sky. And so a few more days went by.

At last one evening he told her about the small split logs and the little brown cottage and the children.

'So!' she said, 'they are cheating me! And I always try to be a good woman to them!'

She spent the evening thinking, sometimes she shook her head and it seemed to Manfred she was in silent conversation with someone he could not see.

'If you're making the tea,' she called out to the girls, 'I'll have a cup of coffee.'

'If I sack one of them, which one do I sack?' she questioned but went on talking before receiving any answer. 'Or do I sack them all? If I sack no one then they will think to go on cheating. Of course you know,' she said to Manfred, 'the woman was never married and the man who was killed was not working for me. They are all thieves,' she said. 'You go to bed,' she said to her nephew. 'I have to sit and think.'

So he tried to sleep in the spacious empty room

which was his and it was as if he kept seeing the men in the clearing working, how clearly he saw them in the jarrah forest.

'There's nothing in the world like a really good woman,' a voice came out into the stillness, and he turned over and turned again trying to sleep.

In the morning they sat facing each other at breakfast. He watched the food going down her thin throat and he found he had no appetite not even for the coffee. He wished he had not told the story to her.

The wind in the perpetually swaying tree tops seemed to sigh with a sadness which was beyond his imagination. Neither of them spoke and then in the stillness of the morning they heard the rumbling of the first trailer. In a few moments it would come along on the other side of the shallow ravine and they would see it pass the open space where the dead tree held up its arms in prayer at all times of the day and night. At once she was at the verandah rail.

'Quick!' she called to her nephew. 'Count the chains! There should be four chains. Regulations you know.' And then she leaned over the rail and screamed at the trailer, 'Thieves! Robbers! You are cheating me! You are all sacked! You won't get away with this!' her voice was lost in the noise of the heavy trailer as it rumbled by in the headlong run to the foundry. Of course the driver, tucked away in the brightly coloured cabin, couldn't hear her, neither could he see her as he had to watch the road and was not able to peer through gaps in the trees.

'There!' she said to Manfred. 'That will teach them not to cheat me!' She sat down again and waved the red enamel coffee pot at him.

'I grind myself,' she said. 'Is good!' After a little time she said, 'You know, it came to me in the night. They wanted me to know about the wood they were giving away. Of course they could not tell me themselves because what could I do then? So what do they do, all night I am thinking it out, they tell you but not exactly, they need not have, they took you there, they could have told you to go on any of the other trucks and never on that one. But, you understand their reason? They wanted to show you so that I would know.'

He hadn't thought of their reason for taking him to the little nut of a cottage, he would never forget that place, left to himself he might never have known why they took him there. His aunt was still talking.

'The woman has to live,' she said. 'In the country one has to help people. There are feckless people who need help all the time, you could give everything to them and they would still need. That is no good. But this woman, this is a different thing. They are good men,' she said. 'And they know I am a good woman.'

Of course his aunt was right, they could have concealed the theft from him, but on purpose they took him to the cottage and let him hear for himself the wood roar from the trailer making those crazy mountains between the almond trees. Now he understood.

He waited till she had screamed her punishment at all the trailers.

'I think I can smell the rain coming,' his aunt turned from the verandah rail.

It was time for him to leave the jarrah forest. He thought he would not be able to bear going away but already it was fading.

'Come again soon,' his aunt said. 'It is healthy here you know.' She thought he had been unwell and for the time being he continued to let her think so. He knew what she meant, there were intangible qualities of light and air and going to bed knowing that, close by, trees were rocking their branches like green cradles and that under the earth their roots were strong and deep. It was a healthy place, he would have liked to stay but it was time for him to go on to other things.

'Next time you come I cook myself,' his aunt said. He felt he didn't know nearly enough about women. Later he would come back and then certainly he would see that he did not neglect the girls.

Ageing, I Thought, Was Something That Happened To Older People
LILY BRETT

Ageing, I thought, was something that happened to older people.

Soon after I moved to New York, I went to a concert by the pianist, Daniel Barenboim, at the Lincoln Center. I was very excited. I'd been playing his recording of Beethhoven's La Pathetique in my Peugeot, everywhere I drove, in Melbourne. It was the first piece of music I had grown to love. It was the only piece of music I listened to.

Listening to music was new to me. For a lot of my life, I couldn't bear to listen to any music, I needed silence. Every time I took the cassette out of its box, I looked at Daniel Barenboim, dark, brooding and handsome, on the cover.

something that happens to other people

Daniel Barenboim came on to the stage to deafening applause. I wasn't the only one who was excited about seeing him. The audience clapped and clapped. I sat there numb. Daniel Barenboim was stocky and grey. When the applause died down, I turned to my husband and said, in a shaky whisper, 'I thought he was dark.'

'We were all dark, once,' my husband said.

I think I thought ageing was something that happened to other people. And, in a way, it does. We are not who we used to be.

I look at photographs of myself at twenty. My hair is ironed straight. I have thick, black eyeliner above and below my eyes. I am wearing a long, psychedelic-patterned dress and bells around my ankles and wrists.

Who was I? What was I thinking? I must have thought I looked great. I remember feeling pleased with my diamante-lined false eyelashes. I remember my father crying when he looked at me. I had painted small, black hearts across my cheekbones.

'What happened to my daughter?' he said. 'Where is my daughter?'

Where was I? I don't know. I was buried under a mountain of pancake make-up, blusher, mascara

ageing, I thought, was something that happened to older people

and lashes. I was also buried under pounds of fat. Fat covered me like a comfortable blanket, except it wasn't very comfortable. It coated me and protected me. I felt encased and safe. Safe from whom? From what? It would take me decades to work that out.

And who was I in another photograph? I am smiling, in a hospital bed. I am dressed in a white lace Victorian nightgown. My hair is parted in the middle. I am holding my newborn son. I am a picture of serenity. Who was I?

I was twenty-two. And all the mess was covered up, as it can be when you're twenty-two, by fearlessness, by innocence, by good skin, good hair and the right shade of lipstick.

My son is twenty-six, now. And he's one of the great joys in my life. Why did I have him? Why did I have an IUD removed, and set out to get pregnant at twenty-one? I had no idea why, then. For years afterwards, I wondered why I so adamantly wanted to have a child. I was a child myself.

I think it had something to do with sabotage. The sabotage of myself. I had a successful career. I was a rock journalist. I'd travelled the world interviewing rock stars. Jimi Hendrix, The Who, The Mamas and Papas, Janis Joplin, Sonny and Cher, The Doors. Everybody who was anybody in the rock world. In Australia, I was also on television and radio. I think the success was too much for me. I couldn't wait to give it all up. Of course, I didn't know I was doing that.

I was so thrilled to give birth to a boy. I was ecstatic. I couldn't believe my luck. I thought our family didn't have boys. I thought they lost boys. My mother lost a son, in the Lodz ghetto. She lost four brothers, in Auschwitz, and she aborted a small boy, in shame, after the war, in Melbourne.

In Guys Hospital, in London, I couldn't sleep. I stayed up for two days and two nights looking, with amazement, at my beautiful boy. Several days later, I was even more amazed. I realised I had to take him home with me.

I hadn't thought further than giving birth to the baby I wanted. I certainly hadn't thought of taking him home. What was I thinking? I think I wasn't thinking.

I wasn't thinking about my mother. Now, I think part of the reason I had my son was my mother. I wanted to give her the sons she'd lost. I wanted to

ageing, I thought, was something that happened to older people

give her some of her family back. I wanted to give her the grandchildren she never dreamt she'd live to see, when she was lying, near-naked, ablaze with typhoid on the frozen ground at Stuthof, where she was sent after Auschwitz.

My baby boy made a big difference to my mother. She fell in love with him. And he fell in love with her. When she introduced him to people, she said, 'my son'. Sometimes, when I was there, she corrected herself, 'My grandson', she would say.

Nine years ago, when she lay dying of cancer, at sixty-four, she wanted him at her side. And he wanted to be there. Did I know about the fierce love that would grow between my mother and my son? The love that would fill gaps and dreams. I don't know.

I didn't know much, then. I didn't know why I got married, the first time around. I married someone I'd met when I was nineteen. He was tall and blond. He was as Aryan as you could get. Later, when his blond hair darkened, I bleached it right back.

The second time I married, I was thirty-four. And I knew why I was getting married. I was crazy about him. I was crazy about a man who was a stranger. I fell in love with him minutes after I met him. What did I know? I knew something. I'm still crazy about him.

Recently, my younger daughter asked me how I could have fallen in love with someone I hardly knew. It was a hard question. I stumbled around, talking about what we unconsciously perceive and understand about each other. But she wasn't satisfied. And she was right. I didn't have an answer.

I don't have an answer to many things. I thought I would. I thought age brought answers. I think it does. But not all the answers.

I have some answers. And so I should. I've spent half my adult life in analysis. Anyone who's read my books will know the head count. Three analysts. Many years.

It has been a crucial part of my life. One that both separated me from others and gave me a greater insight into other lives, as well as my own. For most of those years, I knew no one in analysis. When I began, my mother wept and said I was casting shame over the whole family. My father said he'd heard shocking things about my analyst.

I dedicated my first book of fiction to my second

ageing, I thought, was something that happened to older people

analyst. I named a child after my first, and my next book will be dedicated to my last analyst.

Analysis saved me. It saved me from being the least I could be. It wasn't easy. I've travelled to analysis sessions, early in the morning, four times a week, in different parts of the world. In hot weather, in below-freezing temperatures, in snowstorms and in pouring rain. I've walked, driven and bussed. I've cried gallons of tears. I've wept everywhere it's possible to weep. On the bus, in the car, on the streets.

But, I made it. The better part of me emerged. The part of me that feels entitled to have a life. To live without paying a price. And I'm grateful. So grateful.

I'm surprised at how much gratitude I feel. I feel grateful for things I didn't notice or understand, in the past. A new sense of perspective came with the gratitude.

Last year, in an acceptance speech for an award, I said that my novel, *Just Like That*, was a celebration of love.

A celebration of the lives of my mother and father who survived Auschwitz. And a celebration of the fact that my mother and my father, who lost everyone they loved, in Auschwitz, did not lose the ability to love.

My mother and father survived five years in the Lodz ghetto before being transported to Auschwitz, where they were separated from each other, but not separated from their love for each other. It took them six months after the war to find each other, and they are a rare statistic—two Jewish people who were married to each other before the war, each surviving. I was very lucky to grow up in the middle of that love.

I wrote this speech very soon after being told I had won the award. I knew, and quite surprised myself by how sure I was, that it was my parents' ability to love that saved not only them, after the war, but me. It took me years to see how lucky I was to experience and be the recipient of that love. I spent decades dwelling on what was missing. I spent decades wishing we weren't surrounded by the dead, by past and future Nazis, by anguish and absence.

I'm also surprised at how lucky I am able to feel. Feeling lucky has always felt dangerous. So, I've

ageing, I thought, was something that happened to older people

pre-occupied myself with what's wrong. Once I start thinking about what's wrong, I can shuck off the discomfort that feeling lucky brings.

But, I do feel lucky. Lucky to be married to the man I'm married to. Lucky to have my children. Lucky to have lived long enough to see my children grown up. When they were younger, I dreaded dying before they'd done enough growing. I kept detailed diaries of their childhoods, and of my feelings for them, in case I wasn't around to remind them of their past. It wasn't that I was ill. I never even caught colds, but I did catch the notion of death accompanying love. And, for my parents, that was true. Everyone they were related to died, everyone they loved died.

I allowed myself to feel lucky so rarely that the moments stand out. When my son was small, he said to his best friend, within earshot of his best friend's mother, 'My mother is much nicer than your mother'. I was told this by the mother. When I stopped laughing, I felt very lucky to have a kid who thought that.

I feel lucky to have written the books I've written. I didn't finish high school. I threw my education away. It was only one of the valuable

something that happens to other people

things I discarded. I was in the A-form, at University High School, a school for bright kids, when, seemingly out of the blue, I couldn't understand anything any teacher said. I was sixteen.

I spent the next three years trying to pass the final year of high school. I couldn't read any of the text books. Nothing I read made sense. Words and paragraphs swam around the page. One year I would pass French, Economics and English, the next year I would fail all three and pass something else. Another year, I gave up and went to the movies when some of the exams were on. I never managed to pass the requisite number of the right subjects in the one year.

In retrospect, I realise I was having a nervous breakdown of sorts. Nobody was troubled by it at the time. My parents were bothered, and I think very puzzled, but they had greater concerns about me. I was too fat. I had to lose weight. So, this failing and flailing of a bright, young girl went largely unnoticed. No teacher commented on it. In fact the Economics teacher at University High School said, after I failed Economics the first time around, that he would rather I didn't come back to

ageing, I thought, was something that happened to older people

his class. He said I was a disruption in the classroom.

I was shocked and hurt. I thought I was good at Economics. I used to be, before my decline. How I was a disruption wasn't clear to me. I guessed it must have been my chatting. I was always chatting.

In school photographs, I look bright and cheerful. Over the years, when I've met people I went to University High School with, they tell me they remember me, always cheerful, always laughing. What was I laughing about? Why was I looking so cheerful when I was so clearly in trouble?

I stopped trying to study, and I got a job as a journalist. Boy was I lucky to land that job. At the job interview, no one asked me if I could write. They wanted to know if I had a car. I said, yes, a pink Valiant. I got the job. Soon, I was writing page after page of the newspaper, every week. And I hardly saw my car again.

Feeling lucky still has an edge to it. I don't want to push my luck. So, I filter and dilute my days with odd complaints and aches, and let the heady giddiness of feeling lucky seep in in bits and pieces.

I'm forty-nine, now, and I can feel lucky. Physically, I've changed, too. I'm older and I'm lighter. I weigh less than I did when I was twelve, but I was a bit of a hefty twelve-year-old. I've been regaining my body, which was lost to me for years.

I have years of uncomfortable memories. Me, at nineteen, a rock journalist at the Monterey Pop festival, in California. I'm wearing a nylon orange and yellow spotted dress. The dress is loose, designed to flow around and over my hips. It has short sleeves, that are obviously too tight.

They weren't too tight when I'd last worn the dress, and when I put it on I was shocked and depressed by the fact that the sleeves were strangling my flesh. I'm interviewing Eric Burdon and trying to suck my breath in, as though holding my breath will lessen the width of my arms. It's hot and I feel awful.

The same year. Another scene. I'm interviewing Sonny and Cher, in their house, in Los Angeles. Cher is barely wearing anything. She's all shoulders and midriff and legs. She admires my purple false eyelashes. She asks me where I got them. I can't answer. I'm too distracted by my chafed thighs, red and sore from perpetually brushing against each other.

ageing, I thought, was something that happened to older people

I had succeeded in making my body ugly, and almost obsolete. It seemed my brain was the only part of me I used, and I could have done a better job with that.

I thought fast and spoke with reasonable speed, but everything else about me was slow. I walked slowly. I never played sport. I didn't dance. When I look at photographs of myself, I want to cry. I look awful.

I never looked at my body. After the shower, if I passed a mirror, I'd look the other way. I never touched my body. I thought I was lucky if someone else thought I felt nice.

I created this havoc with myself because of a complicated confluence of history and family. Death camps, starvation, greed, a beautiful mother who'd lost everything except her looks. Oh, it was a heady brew. And I brewed and stewed on it.

I took my looks, regular, symmetrical, attractive features, and I huffed and puffed until I'd distorted myself and resembled somebody else. And, in that other person, I was free to feel peaceful.

Feeling free is not easy for me. Still. 'Freedom was never something you let yourself get away with for very long', my first analyst wrote, in a letter to me, fifteen years ago.

'You're much freer now,' my younger daughter, who is home from college for the weekend, says to me, looking over my shoulder as I type.

'You can dance, too,' she says. 'You never used to dance.'

She's right. I can dance.

'You can get out on the dance floor and have a wonderful time,' she says.

I smile at her.

'You're much calmer, too,' she says. 'It's easier to tell you when I don't like something. I don't think the world will fall apart, or anything.'

I understand exactly what she's saying. She's always been a good kid. Too good. I used to worry that she felt she had to be good. That she felt I had too many demons to deal with without her adding to the distress. Last year, I bought her a T-shirt. It read, 'NO MORE MS NICE PERSON.'

The former Ms Nice Person looks at the title of this piece.

'I think you've gotten older and younger,' she says. 'I think you take more risks than you used to. You're more curious, more confident.'

ageing, I thought, was something that happened to older people

This is my baby who's talking. The child, who, despite the fact that she's 5'8", and in her final year of college, I can't stop feeling is still my small girl.

'Yes,' she looks at me and says. 'You're not so scared of things. You've worked through a lot of sad things. You've worked through the pain of your mother's death, and you've got a great friendship with Grampa. And, you've had the power and strength to finish a very intensive analysis.'

I've stopped writing and am just staring at her. How can she sum up my life like this?

'You growing has helped me to grow up,' she says.

Grown up. I feel grown up. For years I didn't. Now, I can rock and roll to Little Richard, turning and whirling and laughing, and feel very grown up. I have the freedom to be silly, to jump, to ride a bicycle, to not think about what anyone thinks.

This freedom, this ability to feel my body, to use my body, to be excited by my body, started, in very small ways, over a decade ago. It progressed very slowly, more slowly than my analysis, with which it was inextricably woven.

I began by walking. One block, two blocks, three

blocks. It was a foreign experience. I was like my father. He drove the car to the milk-bar, seven houses away.

Our family wasn't big on movement. Movement of the mouth, maybe, but not sport, exercise. Never. Where would that get you? Certainly not into law school, where my parents hoped I was headed.

At Lee Street Primary School, in Carlton, someone suggested I go to gym classes. I was eight years old, and chubby. I went once. A woman told me to swing from a rope. Everyone before me, one by one, had swung from this rope. I couldn't. I couldn't lift my legs off the ground.

I never went back to the gym. I couldn't see why I should. How was swinging from a rope going to help me? Would it help me avoid the sex that went on in the lane after school? I didn't think so. In the afternoons, I walked as fast as I could past whatever poor girl was being fucked, in the lane, by one of the bigger boys in the school. My heart pounded. I held my breath and hoped I was invisible.

It was bad enough being masturbated by one of those big boys, at the school assembly, in the morning. As we sat, cross-legged, on the floor,

ageing, I thought, was something that happened to older people

listening to a teacher speak, many of us girls had boys' hands down our pants. I've often wondered why nobody noticed.

But, it wasn't an age of notice or concern or thought, in many ways. We had kids of all ages in our class. The older kids were there because they couldn't speak English. I remember being frightened by the huge patches of blood that would appear on the back of Ada's dress from time to time. I thought she was dying.

I spent a lot of my time at Lee Street pretending that I wasn't scared. I was counter-phobic. Years later, all the fears would surface, and I would become phobic. A fear of the streets was one of my phobias. Now, I walk the streets of Manhattan. Every day.

Every day, I walk across the Westside Highway to the path along the Hudson River. I power walk. I pump my arms and walk as fast as I can. Five miles a day. It takes me an hour and fifteen minutes. I love it. Some mornings I don't want to stop. I want to walk and walk. When Samuel L. Jackson said, in *Pulp Fiction*, 'I want to walk the earth,' I knew exactly what he meant.

There is a whole life on the Hudson River. There

are ducks and birds. There are tugs and barges and boats and yachts. One morning, the QE2, sailed up, out of nowhere, it seemed, in front of me. There it was, in the pink, early-morning light, as big as a city block, and so close.

There is always traffic on the river. There are police launches and there are ferries, and sometimes there are fishermen. The Statue of Liberty is always there. And is always a moving sight. The air smells of salt, and I breathe in as much of it as I can.

I've made friends on this river path. An elderly Chinese couple wave to me, every day. They jog. In heatwaves and in blizzards. I adore them. They both wave to me with a broad and enthusiastic wave. It's a sweet, and sometimes strange, community of exercisers. There are joggers, runners, walkers, power-walkers, strollers. A young woman I see, most days, passed me her card, in mid-run, last week, and suggested we meet for coffee. I said yes, and then felt nervous. I've nodded to her, daily, for over a year, but don't know her at all. Will we have anything in common over a cafe table? At least I know she drinks coffee. She probably won't

ageing, I thought, was something that happened to older people

have a piece of cake with her coffee. They look a pretty healthy lot these runners.

Something healthy I've been doing for myself, is eating well. It's such a simple phrase, eating well, and it's taken me so long to put it into effect.

I've always eaten strangely. I've been on a diet for most of my life. I've been trying, with varying degrees of desperation, to lose weight since I was ten. My school notebooks were filled with calculations. I would give myself six months to lose two stone. I'd look at the calculations. Two stone in six months. That would be roughly a pound a week. Easy. In fact too easy, I needn't start the diet for another month.

The calculations would continue. Two stone in five months. Still no need to rush into it. Two stone in three months. Still possible. Two stone in one month. I could fast. Two stone in two weeks. Impossible. I'd have to give up. I did these calculations over and over again. I can calculate pounds per stone, and divide that by weeks, faster than anyone I know.

All my notebooks were filled with figures, and I was still fat. Maybe I could be somebody else? I wished I could swap myself for somebody else.

Somebody old, somebody infirm, somebody ugly, it didn't matter, as long as it was somebody slim. How could a young girl want that?

How could I have wanted that? I was so pretty. Huge brown eyes, thick, curly hair. What was wrong with me? The same thing that is wrong with lots of women. I know very few women who aren't preoccupied with their weight. Thin women, average-sized women, overweight women.

My elder daughter, who's worked on and off, part-time, as a waitress, says she rejoices when she sees women who eat heartily and who enjoy their food and their appetite.

I'm always stunned by how complicated the matter of food and their own body-size is to women. Women who would be revolted by one excess pound on their own bodies happily date, and find attractive, fat men.

I'm also a bit stunned by the change in my own eating. From the girl who once thought she'd cure herself of an addiction to Mars Bars by eating as many as she liked—I ate twenty-five in one day, and the feeling that I never wanted to see another Mars Bar lasted two days—I've turned into a person who eats three well-balanced meals a day.

ageing, I thought, was something that happened to older people

I was over forty when I began to change my eating habits. I can't believe that I prefer chicken and vegetables to chocolate. But, I do. If this is sounding all too good to be true, it isn't. I sweated for this. Analysis isn't cheap or easy.

I sweat in other ways, now. Two years ago, at forty-seven, I took up weight-lifting. No one in my family had ever lifted anything heavier than a large cheesecake. Physical strength was not something that our family dwelt on. Although, my parents were very impressed by the fact that I could swim. I learnt to swim at high school. Every time my mother or father saw me swim, they would say to each other, in amazement, and with some pride, 'Look at how she swims'.

I thought I was a pretty good swimmer, too. I was swimming in the Olympic-sized pool at the Beverly Hilton Hotel, in Los Angeles, a few years ago. I was doing my third lap when I heard a man, at the edge of the pool, say to his young daughter, 'Look at her style, look at her style'. I felt very proud. The little girl looked at me. 'Not her,' the father said. 'The woman in the other lane.' I swam the rest of that lap trying not to come up for air.

I don't know what prompted me to want to lift

weights. My need seemed to come right out of the blue. But, I've spent enough hours on analysts' couches to know that nothing comes out of the blue.

I overwhelmed myself by going out and buying some weight-lifting equipment. I asked the man in the store what I needed to begin with. The store sent someone to set the equipment up for me. I found myself a trainer.

At first, I had no chance of bench pressing. I was too scared to lie on the bench. It seemed too narrow. I was sure I'd fall off. But, I didn't. Now, I squat with 150 pounds and can do partial deadlifts with 180 pounds. These are heavy weights. I discovered, years after I came into it, that I have a strong body.

In the beginning, I was mesmerised by my new muscles. I rushed to the bathroom mirror, several times a day, rolled up my sleeves and flexed my biceps. I couldn't believe they were still there.

Weight-lifting has changed the shape of my body. It took me quite a while to get used to the change. I used to wake up, in fright, in the middle of the night. I'd have bumped into myself and not recognised who I was. I'd touched myself and felt

ageing, I thought, was something that happened to older people

a strange body. A body that was a different size, a different texture, a different density.

I love weight-lifting. I love it and love it. I stopped talking about it, to anyone who'd listen, when I heard the strident, evangelical tone in my voice. I wanted everyone I met to lift weights. A Jewish-Polish, born-again, middle-aged iron pumper. Who'd have believed it?

I lift weights three times a week. And I always love it. Even when I'm very tired, and I've had a dismal day. Four reps into a bench press, and I feel much better, and the world looks much better.

It's so easy. You do it three times a week. And that's it. It works. It's not like learning to play the piano. You don't have to practise in between workouts. Lifting weights also increases bone density, which, for women, decreases more sharply at menopause.

I prepared for menopause as I've prepared for most things in my life. I read about it. Half-a-dozen books. I read them years before I needed to, and I was convinced I was undergoing an early menopause.

Did my moods fluctuate, the books asked. Of course they did. Did I cry more? I cried for half of our first year in New York. Did I more easily feel irritable? Less patient? Have headaches? Yes, yes, yes. I decided I was menopausal.

A woman who lives upstairs in our building was menopausal. She told me it was the worst time in her life. She's a warm, intelligent woman and I like her a lot. One day, I met her coming down the staircase. She was sobbing. I asked her if there was anything wrong—a stupid question. 'I was driving my car down MacDougal Street,' she said to me, 'and I came to a police barricade and I drove through it. I knew it was a police barricade,' she wept, 'but I just had to get to the post office.'

'I can understand a need to get to the post office,' I said. It didn't cheer her up. She kept weeping all the way down the stairs.

'At least I'm doing better than she is,' I said to my husband.

'I'm managing my menopause really well,' I said to my elder daughter. And I was. I was swallowing buckets of Evening Primrose Oil and glasses of Motherwort, Chaste Tree and Fresh Valerian Root drops, in water, to counter pre-menstrual and pre-menopausal stress, insomnia and restlessness.

My doctor called to give me the results of the

ageing, I thought, was something that happened to older people

hormone level tests I'd had to determine what stage of menopause I was at.

'Ms Brett,' he said. 'We've got the results. You haven't even begun menopause.'

'No wonder I've been managing it so well,' I said, when I recovered my composure. He didn't laugh.

My husband couldn't stop laughing. I didn't think it was that funny. I'd been battling the irritability, the lack of patience, the headaches, the mood fluctuations. I'd given up tea and coffee.

The next morning I woke up feeling peeved. All that struggle and I wasn't even menopausal. What would the real thing be like?

'I think we're in for a rugged few years,' I said to my husband.

I threw out the Evening Primrose Oil and the Motherwort, Chaste Tree and Fresh Valerian Root. I bought two pounds of freshly ground Colombian coffee, and packets of Earl Grey, English Breakfast and Orange Pekoe tea.

That was a few years ago. Now, I'm well and truly menopausal. Verified by blood tests. Jewish women, I read, statistically experience the worst menopausal symptoms. At least here, in America.

And I was gearing myself up to fit right in with those statistics.

But something happened. I think it was a combination of all those years of analysis—menopause, the change of life, wasn't going to bring me any new revelations, regrets or disturbances, not after examining every detail of every revelation and disturbance—and the walking, the weight-lifting and the eating well.

What happened was an asymptomatic menopause. Yes, no symptoms.

'Do you think I'll get some symptoms?' I asked my gynaecologist.

'Not if you haven't had any up to now,' she said. 'You're well and truly on your way through it.'

Asymptomatic menopause, weight loss, dancing, biceps and triceps. Happy endings, in my own life, make me nervous. I feel the need to say that this is not the perfect life. I feel the need to dredge up difficulties. I'm as imperfect as I ever was, in many ways.

And, not all the damage can be fixed up. I can't get rid of the scars of self-mutilation. One of them runs, vertically, and wildly, down my stomach, the result of an unnecessary emergency appendectomy.

ageing, I thought, was something that happened to older people

I was only ten and wanted to cut all the excitement out of me.

I carry traces of the welts that dotted my teenage legs, red and inflamed, when I was too young to understand how distressed I was. The welts used to itch and itch. And I would scratch and scratch. I've made myself sad thinking about this. Sadness is always a good antidote for too much happiness, for me.

Some things don't change. No matter how much you think you've changed. No matter how much clarity, wisdom, maturity you may feel you've achieved. I can feel the same hurt I felt as a teenager, at a friendship not turning out to be what I imagined it was.

Friendship, deep friendship, a subject that has preoccupied me for most of my life, has, in a strange way, eluded me. I still have the occasional fantasy of the best friend. The friend who shares everything with me. The friend with whom I'm completely connected. Connected to each other, to each other's partners, to each other's children, to each other's pasts. I still long for that sometimes.

Maybe what I'm longing for is the passionate, unbridled friendship of more youthful years. Those years when you don't wait until you feel good, or look good, or it's an opportune and not inconvenient moment to call and see each other. Maybe I long for the unguarded, more truthful, less competitive friendship of the young.

I've tried to put my version of a best-friend friendship into effect, a couple of times, in the past few years, but, of course, it hasn't worked. The women involved had no idea what they were in for.

A new friend, who lives in Washington, said she liked me instantly, because, as she put it to her husband, 'she suffers'. I can understand criteria like that.

My husband doesn't understand my need for friends. He's never wanted a best friend. I am his best friend. He points out that we have lots of friends. Maybe I don't understand my need, either. Despite the thousands of hours I've spent lying on analysts' couches, there's much that I don't understand, and possibly much that I haven't faced.

The city of New York forces me to face others and myself in a way that no other place I've been to does. When I first moved here, I wept each time I passed a homeless person. I looked at the homeless and I saw myself. I looked at the men, and an occasional woman, sleeping in doorways and on park benches, and I saw pictures of Jews dying in the streets, in the Lodz ghetto.

I cooked huge vats of soup for City Harvest, an organisation that picks up food and delivers it to the homeless. I cooked lentil soup with large chunks of beef. I put pork into the split-pea soup. I thickened the soups with a roux and seasoned them carefully.

The first time I did this, I waited for someone to call me up and tell me how delicious the soups were. I felt let down when no one called. And then I felt foolish. What did I think I was doing? Cooking for a dinner party?

Just before the pick-up, I'd stopped myself from writing a list of ingredients on each of the hundred and fifty containers of soups. It dawned on me, at the last minute, that this was not a group of people who'd be scanning labels for the percentage of fat or fibre in their food.

My husband saw the labels I'd started writing. He looked sad.

'I don't think this will be the allergic to wheat, lactose intolerant, additive averse, vegetarian crowd,' he said.

I laughed. 'I must be crazy,' I said.

There are crazy people on the streets of New York. On every street, it seems, some days. They talk. Mainly to themselves. A young man, who was around a lot last summer, carried a yellow, plastic toy telephone with him. He shouted into this telephone as he walked the streets of Soho. At first, I was frightened of him. Frightened by his intensity, and unnerved by the yellow, plastic telephone cord that trailed behind him.

One day, he followed me for four blocks. I don't think he really followed me. I think we were both just going in the same direction. His shouting drowned out my thoughts. I listened to him. Business strategies were flying in to the yellow handset, which he had gripped firmly to his ear. He made intricate social arrangements, and he argued about politics and love. I admired his eloquence, and felt grateful for my sanity.

I, also, like everyone else living in New York, have to face the racial inequalities, and the racial tension. It may feel uncomfortable to face this, but it's healthier than being able to pretend that it doesn't exist.

New York is not like Los Angeles, where you

ageing, I thought, was something that happened to older people

can go from the valet parking in your apartment building to the valet parking at the supermarket or the restaurant. No, here, in New York, you have to inhale the carbon monoxide, and it's good for you.

The weather in New York City is as volatile as the population. Oppressive heat, bitter cold. And there's no way to avoid it. You have to walk in New York. You walk to your destination. To the subway, to the bus stop, to find a taxi.

And the weather changes are so dramatic. I've often been frightened by changes in weather. Before I moved here, news of impending heavy rain unnerved me. As though nature was about to unleash a catastrophe. Catastrophes were on my mind a lot, then. I kept expecting them. And, seemed to spend a lot of time either averting or inviting one.

Now, I've had to adjust to snowstorms and arctic temperatures, and stifling heat and one hundred per cent humidity. Last week, this adjustment was severely tested. The weather forecast said a storm warning watch was in effect. A lot of snow was expected. This forecast soon changed to a blizzard alert.

I hear the words warning, watch, alert, with more

drama than the meteorologist intended. I have to remind myself that this is not the war, just the weather.

And what weather it was. It snowed and snowed. Big, fat, wild, spinning snowflakes thickening the air. You couldn't see where you were. It kept snowing all day and all night. I stood at our windows, for hours, watching the performance.

By the next day, the snowstorm is called The Blizzard of '96, and it's the largest snowfall in New York since 1947. It is still snowing. I've braved the snow to go to the store for supplies, a couple of times. I feel it is the war.

'We've got enough food in the house to eat well for a month,' my husband says. I go out, again. To buy toilet paper. So did lots of other New Yorkers. Supermarkets and smaller stores were depleted of most of their perishable items, and their toilet paper, within hours of the forecast.

The State of New York is declared to be in a state of emergency. I'm strangely calm about this. Well, it is my area of expertise. I've been directing and dissecting emergencies, in my head, for years. I go out to buy some more toilet paper. I step into

ageing, I thought, was something that happened to older people

knee-deep snow. When I come back, I count the rolls of toilet paper on my shelves. Fifty-four.

Later in the day, the snow eases. I tell my husband that I want to walk. My need to walk is very strong. It seems to have replaced my need for Mars Bars, chocolate, chatting on the phone, cooking too much and shopping.

I know I won't be able to do my five miles, but Mayor Guiliani has said that snow ploughs are already out, clearing some of the main streets. My husband says he'll come with me.

We walk, very slowly. The streets are deserted. It is so quiet. A lone skier glides down the middle of West Broadway. We get to the Hudson River. The river looks extraordinary. Large, round, flat slabs of ice are nudging each other, covering the surface of the Hudson like a cracked jigsaw puzzle. The ice forms the same shapes as the congealed fat on top of chilled chicken soup. I'm mesmerised.

We walk back through Tribecca. No one is out. I feel bold. An adventurer. At one with the elements. I plunge my legs into the snow, with pride. I'm not scared.

A woman and a young girl come out of a building. It's still snowing and I have a large cap on. I see them out of the corner of my eye. I look up and notice that they are mother and daughter, and that they're wearing matching fur hats.

The woman calls out, 'hello'. It's a loud and enthusiastic hello. The hello of a fellow traveller. A bonding hello. The hello of those of us who are not cowed by some snow. 'Hello,' I call back. The woman laughs with pleasure. She has a radiant laugh. She really is not scared of this snow. Then, I recognise the blonde hair and the big smile. It's Bette Midler. I smile at her, again. Us Jewish girls are tougher than you think, I think.

Well, Daniel Barenboim is grey. But, I'm always going to be dark. I decided that when I was forty, and the first few grey hairs began to show. Daniel Barenboim obviously didn't make the same decision.

notes on contributors

Glenda Adams is the author of *The Hottest Night of the Century, Games of the Strong, Dancing on Coral* (winner of the Miles Franklin Award and the NSW Premier's Award) and *Longleg* (winner of the National Book Council Banjo Award and the *Age* Fiction Book of the Year Award). She was born and educated in Sydney and spent many years teaching in New York before returning to Australia, where she teaches fiction writing at the University of Technology, Sydney. Her latest book is *The Tempest of Clemenza*, published by HarperCollins in 1996.

Lily Brett is the author of five collections of poetry and three books of fiction. Her first book, *The Auschwitz Poems*, won the 1987 Victorian Premier's Award for Poetry and both her fiction and poetry have won other major prizes, including the 1995 NSW Premier's Award for fiction. A new volume of poetry will be published in 1997 together with her first non-fiction book. Lily Brett is married to David Rankin. They have three children and live in New York.

Sara Dowse was born in Chicago, lived as a child in New York and then Los Angeles. In 1958 she came to Australia, settling first in Sydney, and ten years later moved to Canberra where she still lives. She worked in publishing and as a journalist before joining the Prime Minister's Department in 1974 to head its newly-created women's affairs section, which under her leadership became the Office of Women's Affairs, now the Office of the Status of Women. Her first novel, *West Block*, was published in 1983, followed by *Silver City* in 1984. She co-authored *Canberra Tales* with her colleagues in Seven Writers; the first edition of this collection was published in 1988 and in 1996 was reissued under the title *The Division of Love*. A third novel, *Schemetime*, appeared in 1990, followed by *Sapphires* in 1994 and *Digging* in 1996. She is currently working on a biography of a great aunt who disappeared in Stalin's purges.

Elizabeth Jolley grew up in the Midlands of England and has been living in Australia since 1959. Her many prize-winning books include *Palomino, The Well, Miss Peabody's Inheritance,*

The Sugar Mother, My Father's Moon, Cabin Fever and *The Georges' Wife*. Her work is published widely overseas and frequently broadcast on the BBC. Her most recent book, *The Orchard Thieves*, was published by Penguin in September 1995. She teaches in the School of Communication and Cultural Studies at Curtin University, Perth, WA.

Joanna Murray-Smith is a playwright, screenwriter and novelist who would love to say that she divides her time between New York and Melbourne. Her novel *Truce* was published by Penguin in 1994.

Georgia Savage was born in Tasmania but has lived most of her life in Victoria. She has published five novels, many short stories and the odd newspaper article about football. Now in her late sixties, she was recently told by a cardiologist that she has the physical fitness of a forty-five-year-old. Although Georgia adheres to a strict regime of diet and exercise, she believes no one will have good health and a youthful spirit without loving companionship and daily doses of laughter.

Roberta B. Sykes, founder and National Executive Officer (Hon.) of Black Women's Action in Education Foundation, works as a consultant, educator and political commentator. A Harvard University graduate and author of five books, she is in frequent demand as a speaker at national and overseas venues. She has won numerous awards, including the 1994 Australian Human Rights Medal for her life's work. Her alter-ego, Bobbi, is a poet with two published anthologies.

Elisabeth Wynhausen is feature writer and columnist who has worked on the *Bulletin*, the *National Times*, the Melbourne *Age* and the Sydney *Sun-Herald*. Long resident in the United States, where her articles appeared in many newspapers and magazines, she has returned to live in Sydney and is a senior writer on the *Australian*. She has published a memoir, *Manly Girls* (1989).

A Woman of Air
Margaret Packham Hargrave

They give me injections and the pain recedes, so I let my dreams take charge of me . . . Time shifts and memory is like a reflection in water that can be disturbed by a fish, a ripple or a stone thrown by a child. I no longer know what it was I lived and what I dreamed. My life is a fantastic lace of lies and dreams, and which is which I can no longer tell . . .

Daphne is dying. As her life ebbs away and she drifts in and out of consciousness, she looks back over her life from childhood to old age, now unable to distinguish between reality and the rich fantasy world she often inhabited.

Determined from an early age to make her mark on the world as a star of stage and screen, Daphne finds herself continually thwarted by the restrictions of suburbia, the demands of her family and the stigma of epilepsy. Can her dreams sustain her life?

'*A Woman of Air* is a highly polished and memorable novel. Hargrave's prose fizzes with both the joy of life and its concurrent strain of sadness. Daphne's story could have been a melancholic one, but through the author's use of delicate humour—at times uproarious—the tale becomes a celebration.'

MATTHEW CONDON

Motherlove
Edited by Debra Adelaide

Only two things were clear after both births: that my body had just performed the most extraordinary miracle, and that I would never be the same again.

Motherlove is a collection of stories written by women about birth, their babies and their lives beyond the moment of childbirth, when the world changed forever. Sometimes funny and practical, sometimes sad and moving, these stories will enthrall and delight.

The first collection of its kind, *Motherlove* is for anyone who has ever observed or experienced the unique and complicated pleasures of having a child.

Debra Adelaide
Gabrielle Carey
Anna Maria Dell'oso
Noni Hazlehurst
Dorothy Johnston
Fiona Place
Pat Mamajun Torres
Brenda Walker
Sue Woolfe

Anna Booth
Julie Clarke
Sara Dowse
Adele Horin
Mary Moody
Annette Stewart
Monica Trapaga
Rachel Ward

Women/Love/Sex
edited by Susan Johnson

In this riveting companion anthology to *Men/Love/Sex*, Australia's leading women writers and most exciting new names lay bare their feelings about love and sex. Painfully honest, confronting, lyrical and poignant, *Women/Love/Sex* reveals just what women talk about when they talk about love.

Contributors include:
Candida Baker
Helen Barnes
Carmel Bird
Ann Dombroski
Justine Ettler
Marion Halligan
Dorothy Hewett
Chloe Hooper
Lyn Hughes
Cathy Coote
Kathleen Stewart
Jane Hyde
Susan Johnson
Gabrielle Lord
Gillian Mears
Maurilia Meehan
Sally Morrison
Francesca da Rimini
Penelope Rowe
Mandy Sayer
Amy Witting
Sue Woolfe

Leaning Towards Infinity
Sue Woolfe

This is not my story.

It is the story of Frances Montrose, an Australian woman with no formal mathematics training who carried across the world, in a borrowed suitcase bulging with a friend's balldresses, something no one knew about.

The discovery of a new number.

I can barely add up so I can't tell you much about her mathematics. Only to say she was a genius. And she was my mother, my love, my emptiness. Her mathematics was her secret passion and her curse. And my curse too.

HYPATIA MONTROSE

'With this book, Sue Woolfe places herself amongst the finest of Australian writers. It is a tale refreshing in its combination of devices, cunning but calm in the telling, and full of valid revelation. I would not be surprised if it became a cult book of great durability.'

TOM KENEALLY

'Tremendously original and inventive.'

KATE GRENVILLE

Welcome Back
Thea Welsh

A wickedly funny novel about the consequences—for other people—of one woman's deception.

When socially ambitious upstart Janey Taylor is made president of Sydney's most elite charity committee, tongues start wagging. But this is Janey's one shot at the big time and she's determined to be a huge success.

First she has to find someone very, very famous—and quite above reproach—to be the guest-of-honour at the most important social event of the year, the glamorous Goldfish Ball.

When the committee hits upon the idea of inviting screen legend Mara Haines, everyone agrees she's the perfect choice. Mara has become famous all over again as the star of America's most popular TV series, she mixes in international society, and she supports worthy causes. But, best of all, she's told the world she was born in Tasmania.

There's just one small problem.

Mara Haines might be the Apple Isle's favourite daughter, but she's never even set foot in the place.

The discovery of this awful truth threatens Janey Taylor's future but the situation is out of her control . . . a lot of people have a stake in Mara Haines' past.

'I can't remember a better Australian first novel.'
Independent Monthly reviewing Thea Welsh's Banjo-winning novel *The Story of the Year of 1912 in the Village of Elza Darzins*.